Flora Pauline Wilson Kopta

Bohemian Legends

Second Edition

Flora Pauline Wilson Kopta

Bohemian Legends
Second Edition

ISBN/EAN: 9783744714303

Printed in Europe, USA, Canada, Australia, Japan

Cover: Foto ©Andreas Hilbeck / pixelio.de

More available books at **www.hansebooks.com**

BOHEMIAN LEGENDS AND

OTHER POEMS

BY

F. P. KOPTA

SECOND EDITION

NEW YORK:
WILLIAM R. JENKINS,
1896.

DEDICATED

TO

VOJTA NÁPRSTEK, ESQ.,

CHIEF OF THE CITY COUNSEL OF PRAGUE.

INTRODUCTION

TO THE SECOND EDITION.

BOHEMIAN literature is hardly known; indeed, many people do not even know that such a literature exists at all. Of late some praiseworthy efforts have been made by Mr. Wratislaw, M.A. (late fellow of Christ College, Cambridge), and some French writers, to rescue from oblivion at least something of Bohemian literature. In his own words (*Literature of Bohemia*, George Bell Co. 1878), he says: "And at the present time the people of Great Britain are for the most part in a similar state of ignorance with regard to the literature of Bohemia, scarcely believing indeed that it has any literature at all, and utterly at a loss to account for that great intellectual and religious revolution, which, in the beginning of the fifteenth century, shook the power of Rome to its foundation, and animated a Slavonic people of only four millions to maintain successfully a single-handed conflict against the Papacy and the German empire for full two hundred years. And if it yielded at length to overwhelming numbers and weight, it was not until it had been undermined for nearly a century by the crafty and cruel policy of scions of the Hapsburg dynasty upon its throne. * * * It is a very unfortunate circumstance that so much of Bohemian literature has been lost, or rather ruthlessly destroyed by the emissaries and agents of the Church of Rome. * * * It mattered little to such barbarians whether any work that fell into their clutches was of Catholic or Protestant tendency, if it were but in the detested Bohemian tongue, and one Jesuit boasted on his death-bed that he had destroyed with his own hands no less than sixty thousand volumes in that language." I would also mention a very valuable collection of translations made from the Bohemian by the celebrated English linguist, Dr. John Bowring (Výbor z básnictví Českého, Cheskian Anthology). Being a history of the poetical literature of Bohemia, with translations by Dr. John Bowring (London, 1832: Rowland Hunter). He also in his introduction explains why Bohemia has so little literature, and also, in a way, why it never can have. Writing of the battle of Bílá Hora, he says: "Though the battle of the White Mountain, in 1620, was fatal only to the reformers of Bohemia, yet its consequences were terrible to the whole Bohemian people. Civil war in its worse shape devastated the land, and so fierce were its visitations that the Jesuit Balbin, in one of his letters, expresses his surprise that after so many proscriptions, exiles, flights, and suffering, a single inhabitant should remain. The language of Bohemia was abandoned—its literature fell into decay. The taint of heresy had so deeply stained the works of more than two centuries, that they were all recklessly condemned to the flames. Banishment was the portion of the most illustrious among the Bohemians, and equal, undistinguishing malediction pursued everything which bore a Slavonian character. Legends of the saints, trumpery discussions about trumpery dogmas—and all those streams of pitiful and useless learning, in which civil and religious despotism seek to engage and exhaust inquiry, were poured over Bohemia." * * * "An ingenuous criticism on the popular poetry of the Bohemians may be seen in the *Prague Monthly Periodical* (August, 1827), written by M. Müller, the æsthetic professor, in that capital. There is truth in the observation, that history and heroism have furnished few subjects for the Bohemian national songs, and, he says, is the more remarkable when they are compared or contrasted with those of other Slavonian races, especially the Servian and the Russian. But how should such songs exist—or rather if they ever existed, how should they be long preserved in a state of society where no man dares to be a Bohemian? That freedom of thought and expression which opens to the poet the great expanse of space and time—the whole field of the past and the future—which allows him to revel in all that is delightful in recollection, and in all that is beautiful in anticipation—is denied to the minstrel of Bohemia. He may neither record the struggles of his ancestors for liberty, nor dream of the day when self-government shall give to his country whatever of happiness she is capable of enjoying. Love, of all the passions which he is permitted to sing, is that which allows the widest scope to his imagination—and love is the ever-ruling subject of his verse. And surely their popular poets have treated this subject with exquisite tenderness and effect." These are the opinions and words of two Englishmen, who trod before me the thorny path of Bohemian literature. Had their works been published in Austria, the same fate that met my book, " Bohemian Legends and Ballads," would have met them. They would have been confiscated. Dr. John Bowring, speaking of poor Hanka, says: "It is to be hoped that no impediment will be thrown in his way, which one cannot but fear, from the arbitrary suppression of the fifth volume of his collection. It is not much to allow, that those who have no hope of the future may be permitted to indulge in the memories of the past." This sin I committed, and so my poor little book was confiscated. I can only say that the pub-

lishers, Jansky & Co, placed it before the proper
authorities and received permission to publish it;
about three months after, when it had been publicly
sold all over Austria, it was suddenly confiscated on the
22d of June, 1890. At first I was told it was on account of the poem " John Huss," but in about two weeks
I received the written explanation that it was on account of " The Patriots." The Austrian government
did not confiscate my poem because it was historically
untrue, but because they said that, " one could think
that Ferdinand had acted on the advice of his father
confessor." Here I beg to say that such a thought
never entered my head, and that I agree with William
Coxe, F.R.S., F.A.S. (*Coxe's House of Austria, Bohn's
Standard Library*, p. 181, Pelzel, pp. 731-742):
" Several native and Catholic writers endeavor to exten-
uate the cruelty of Ferdinand, by declaring that he
was with difficulty induced to make these dreadful examples; and was overborne by the representations of his
ministers and the Jesuits. Admitting this fact, it is no
exculpation of his conduct to assert that he acted un-
justly by the advice of his ministers. But the preced-
ing and subsequent transactions, as well as the general
character, the relentless disposition, and the deep-rooted
prejudices of Ferdinand, furnish ample evidence that
he wanted no external impulse to commit acts of
persecution and cruelty against the Protestants."
There is also another poem that may want an explanation, and that is, Kryspek's " Goblet." It will be found
in *Coxe's House of Austria*, Vol. II., p. 180. " Three
months elapsed without the slightest act of severity
against the insurgents of Bohemia. Many, lulled into
security by the dreadful calm, emerged from their hiding places, and the greater part remained quiet at
Prague. But in an evil hour all the fury of the tempest
burst upon their heads. Forty of the principal insur-

gents were arrested in the night of the 21st of January,
1621, and after being imprisoned four months, and
tried before an imperial committee of inquiry, twenty-
three were publicly executed, their property confiscated,
the remainder either banished or condemned to perpet-
ual imprisonment. Nor were these examples confined
only to those who had been openly concerned in the re-
bellion, for a mandate of more than inquisitorial severity
was issued, commanding all landholders who had
participated in the insurrection to confess their delin-
quencies, and threatening the severest vengeance if they
were afterward convicted. This dreadful order spread
general consternation; not only those who had shared
in the insurrection acknowledged their guilt, but even
the innocent were driven by terror to self-accusation;
and above seven hundred nobles and knights, almost
the whole body of the landholders, placed their names
on the list of proscription. *By a mockery of the very
name of mercy*, the emperor granted to these unfortunate victims their lives. and honors, which
they were declared to have forfeited by their own
confession; but gratified *his vengeance* and rapacity
by confiscating the whole or part of their property, and thus reduced many of the most loyal and
ancient families to ruin, or drove them to seek a refuge
from their misfortunes in exile or death." The bodies
of the Kryspek family can still be seen in Kralovice.
They were among those who preferred to die rather
than wait to be perhaps tortured or driven from their
country as beggars. As to the interview between Ferdinand and his confessor, it is historically true, and the
whole account can be found in *Histoire Guerre de
Trente Ans*, 1618 and 1648, par E. Charvériat Tome
premier, p. 251, Paris, 1878. "Ferdinand passa sans
repos la nuit qui précéda la signature. Le lendemain

matin, il demanda a son confesseur, le Père Lamormain, s'it pouvait, sans blesser sa conscience condamner
ou faire grâce. Lamormain lui ayant répondu qu'il
avait le droit de faire l'un et l'autre, l'Empereur signa
l'arrêt de mort de vingt-huit des condamnés, la plupart
anciens directeurs." My own poem is founded on an
old chronicle published in Amsterdam. To those who,
having read my poor book, may feel an interest in
Bohemian history, I take the liberty to name the works
from which I drew my information: *Grube Geschichts-
bilder*, p. 195, Leipzig; *Coxe's House of Austria,
Bohn's Standard Library*, London, 1877; *Persécutions
des Patriotes Bohêmes*, 1621; *D'après la Chronique*,
Amsterdam, 1648, p.48; *Histoire Guerre de Trente Ans,*
1618 and 1648, par E. Charvériat, Paris, 1878; *History
of Germany*, by Markham, London, 1876; *The Weltge-
schichte von Moritz Heger and Moritz Schlimpert*,
Dresden, 1856, p. 502; *Geschichte des Dreissigjährigen
Kriegs*, Schiller, Leipzig, 1868, p. 61; *La Bohême*, par
Joseph Friez and Louis Leger, Paris, 1867 (this work
is also forbidden in Austria); *Chants Heroiques et
Chansons, Populaires des Slaves de Bohême*, par Louis
Leger, Paris, 1866; *The Native Literature of Bohemia
in the Fourteenth Century*, by A. B. Wratislaw, M.A.,
London, 1878.*

Trusting that my book may do something toward
making Bohemian literature better known, I send my
poor little book out into the wide world of intellectual
thought, feeling sure that all will sympathize with my
effort, and that some may even feel pleasure in reading
the songs of long ago.

F. P. KOPTA.

---

* There is also a translation of some Bohemian songs by a Mrs.
Robinson, New York, 1850 (I have never been able to get the
book); *Chansons populaires de la Bohême*, Prague, 1854, by Karel
Erben; Bodianski, Moscow, 1887; Ludevít Stúr, Prague, 1853.

CONTENTS.

POEMS—SONGS.

BOHEMIAN LEGENDS.

"BOHEMIA."

Bohemia! land of far renown,
  Well known in the days of old,
From out thy villages and towns
  Came forth thy stalwart sons and bold,
To fight for freedom, and for God,
  Not caring if they bled or died,
If they won liberty to laud
  God on their native mountain side.

Bohemia! that so many years
  Sent out the learned of the earth;
Bohemia, that with many tears
  Passed through the Scripture's second birth;
Thy children, now in history's page,
  Read thy loved name, with beating heart.
In vain thy enemies they rage,
  They cannot dim thy glorious part.

Bohemia! from thy mountains wild,
  God called His martyrs for the truth,
Fiery Jerome and Huss the mild,
  Here wandered in their days of youth.
Here Žižka, with undaunted face,
  Though old and blind, thy warrior son,
Left traces one cannot efface
  Until with history one is done.

Bohemia! there is not an art
  In which thy sons have not excelled;
Thy wares were sold in every mart,
  And praise from enemies compelled.

Now Brožík, with a painter's skill,
  From history has awaked the dead.
Bohemia, that has great men still,
  Nor are thy days of glory fled.

Thy poets, too, have sung thy praise,
  In verses that shall never die.
In many lands one hears the lays
  From Dvořák, like a homeward sigh.
Palacký, with a lover's zeal,
  Has writ thy history great in fame.
Tomek has made us know and feel,
  Though changed, that Prague is still the same.

Brave land, so crushed that still can live
  And teach thy sons the way to fame;
Strong land that still has strength to give
  Men that no enemy can tame.
Thy sons have wandered far and wide;
  One finds them scattered in all lands—
In forests where the black bear hide,
  And amidst Africa's burning sands.

Bohemia! thou hast been my home,
  And I will sing thy praises still.
Wherever 'tis my fate to roam
  No other land thy place shall fill.
Memory shall wander back at will
  Amidst thy forests and thy fields,
And I shall see each well-known hill,
  And listen to the echo's peals.

Bohemia! be thou blest of God—
  May He uphold thee in His strength;
May all thy children learn to laud
  Their father's God, throughout thy length.
Forget not how your fathers fought—
  For what they lived—for what they died;
Remember what your fathers taught,
  And hold to it whate'er betide.

JOHN HUSS.

Oh, mother earth, this son of thine
   Was worthy of the highest place,
And though his ashes in the Rhine
   Were thrown, he lives still in his race.
A dauntless soul that spoke the truth,
   When all the world in darkness slept;
Bohemia's martyred son in sooth
   Blanched not, though friends around him wept.

" Whom should I fear? The Emperor's pass
   Promises liberty and peace."
But still his friends said: " Alas!
   We much misgive us of that peace."
" Whom should I fear then? Those who kill
   The body, but have no more power
Over the soul that triumphs still,
   And conquers in the dying hour?"

" Nay, weep not, I must go from hence,
   - I must speak out the words of God;
I must make out my own defense,
   And prove it by the word of God;
I will come back without the blot
   Of heresy upon my name;
Then blessed, forsooth, will be my lot,
   And great indeed Bohemia's fame."

He went in faith—he went in hope—
   And prison walls, and dungeon cell,
And torture of the chain and rope,
   Were his in that far land as well.
They would not listen to his speech;
   Unheard, he was condemned to die.
In vain he cried, " I do beseech—
   Oh, listen to me ere I die."

Worn down by prison and by pain,
   Denied a counsellor for his cause,
He called on God to help again
   His servant in the general pause.
He was condemned, they listened not
   To words of his, however plain.
What cared those priests for truth? I wot
   They scorned him in their proud disdain.

They placed the cap upon his brow,
   Painted with devils strange and wild,
And tortured him—yes, even now—
   With gibe and curse, at which he smiled.
With eyes upturned he prayed to God,
   Till his brave voice was hushed for aye.
No greater martyr fled to God,
   Than he they burnt upon that day.

They burned him—yes that spirit high
   Was borne to God, by fiery wings;
Praying for them he rose on high,
   Released from all these worldly things.
He has no statue in the land
   Where he was born, and loved so well;
But in the hearts of a small band,
   His ever living memory dwells.

Oh, mother earth, this son of thine
   Was worthy of the highest place.
Oh, yes, Bohemia, he is thine,
   Born of thy own heroic race.
Oh, Christian world, he too is thine,
   A martyr for the Christian faith.
Oh, God of gods, he now is thine,
   Who died for Thee, and in Thy faith.

A HUSSITE SONG.

Attributed to John Žižka.

You who are champions of God,
    And of his law,
Pray Him to assist you, and laud
    Him and His law.
So shall ye conquer through God,
    And be victorious.

Our Lord has told us not to fear
    Those who can kill
The body, but keep Him near,
    And fight with will.
Fight valiantly then with no fear,
    And make strong your hearts.

Christ will repay thee hundredfold—
    For he has said,
" Who dies for me, and in my fold,
    Is happy dead.
For him shall open joys untold—
    And life eternal."

So archers, and lancers, and all
    Ye warlike men;
Hallebards, and ye that appall
    The hearts of men;
Remember all, ye warriors tall,
    God's loving kindness.

E'en if the enemy be strong—
    Still do not fear.
Let God's word be your battle song,
    Know He is near.
Fly not, but fight the battle long,
    Better death than flight.

In the old time they used to say,
    " With a good Lord.
The expedition would make way,
    And with his Lord
His servant would be great one day."
    This remember all.

Ye wagoners, and fiery youth,
    Think of your souls.
Risk not your lives for things, forsooth—
    For wealth untold.
Fight not for plunder, but the truth,
    The truth of your God.

Remember the words of command
    You have been told.
Obey your leader's voice and hand,
    And be ye bold.
Keep your own places in the band,
    Without disorder.

Then joyfully call out, and shout,
    The enemy,
With God's aid, we will surely rout
    Our enemy.
God is our Lord, be that our shout,
    Kill, kill, no quarter.

*TO THE MEMORY

OF THE FORTY SEVEN PATRIOTS EXECUTED AFTER THE BATTLE OF BÍLÁ HORA, JUNE 21, 1621.

It was all over now, all over now—
The battle had been fought and sadly lost,
The battle of the Bílá Hora lost;
And with it died all freedom and all hope.
From henceforth torture and the hangman's rope
Should rule, united with the Jesuit power,
To make the poor Bohemians rue the hour
They dared to listen to the Holy Word;
Or gaze upon His face, whom prophets heard
Pronounced to be the very Son of God.
Let there be silence now—or those who laud,
Pray to the Virgin, or the blessed saints,
Or sink in torture, till the body faints,
Broken and torn, and lets the soul escape;
Yea, like a bird caught in a trap escape.
Ah me, that year of sixteen twenty-one,
Saw many an evil, bloody work well done;
The death of those who were the noblest born—
A country ruined, and a land forlorn,
A noble people made a tyrant's slave,
And their faith hidden in a martyr's grave,
While priestly darkness filled the land like night.

It was all over now, all over now—
And shred and torn, the poor Bohemian land
Lay down to die amidst the conqueror's band,
While all her noblest sons were called to die;
And thanks be unto God, without a sigh
They left this world, for better homes on high.

---

* From a chronicle published in Amsterdam, 1648. Confiscated by the Austrian government, June 22, 1890.

'Tis said the Emperor Ferdinand had qualms—
Perhaps he knew that death would place the palms
Of martyrdom upon those fearless souls and true,
Who preferred death to lives of bitter rue;
Howe'er it be, he passed a restless night,
Tossing and fuming till the dawn of light,
And then he turned him to his ghostly shade,
Father Lamormain, as one half afraid,
And questioned him, if he could do this thing.
" Without hurt to his conscience, or a sting
Of self-remorse, he could condemn to die,
These men?" To which the Jesuit made reply,
" He was the king and could do as he willed;"
And so he signed the warrant, his mind filled
With the great things a king alone can do.

It was the twenty-first of June; the sun
   Rose in its splendor, shining on the land,
And on their faces who would soon have done
   With earthly things, that poor devoted band.
Many were there who in the bygone days
   Had stood before the throne in royal state.
Many were there who trod in learning's ways,
   Whom God had chosen for a martyr's fate.
One gazing out upon the rising sun,
   Beheld a rainbow shining in the sky,
Called to his brethren, " See our faith hath won
   A sign from Heaven. God will see us die,
And from the scaffold we will go to Him,
   Who is alone, the only Truth and Way."
And on their knees they fell and prayed to Him,
   Whom they should see this very blessed day.
'Tis sad to think they could not even pray
   In peace, but pestered by the Jesuit band,
Their last farewells, they could not even say.
   And this, my friends, was by the king's command.
At length the cannons from the Vyšehrad
   Began to fire, that the hour was near,
And meekly praying that God's staff and rod
   Might be their stay, they bid each other " cheer."
Yea, with calm voice, they said, " Oh, brothers ours,
   Ye enter first the paradise of God,
But we will follow in a few more hours.
   Oh, tell our Father that His name we laud."

And those who went to death said, "Have no care;
  God's holy angels will be sent to show
Your souls the way to God, and we shall wear
  The wedding garments ere the sun be low."
The first to die, had been a mighty lord,
  Joachim Andreas Slik, count of Bazan.
Ah, me! ah, me! that fearless soul had soared
  With love of country, and the Count Pason,
As patriot and heretic, must die—
  And his brave hands be nailed up as a sign,
That henceforth none should ever question why
  Their ruler's voice came from across the Rhine.
He gazed upon the shining sun and said,
  "Leave me in peace" (to Jesuit priests that came
To torture his brave soul before it fled),
  "The Sun of Righteousness shall rise the same,
In God's good time, to scatter from our land
  The shadows of this world. We will be free."
And then he knelt upon the wooden stand
  And prayed to God that every one could see.
And it is said a radiance not its own
  Shone in his face, as there he knelt to pray;
And from the scaffold, to a golden throne,
  The count of Pason passed this summer day.
The next to die had walked in learning's ways—
  Václav Budoec, well-known throughout the world
For learned books, that sought from out the maze
  Of darkness still God's banner to unfurl.
'Twas he who said with voice that knew no fear,
  "I'd rather die than see my country die;
And ye have longed so for our butchery here,
  I fain would satisfy you—see me die."
To which the monks replied, "We fain would show
  An erring soul the way to Heaven's gate."
Then smilingly he told them, "Is that so?"
  Then quickly answer ere it be too late.
With many questions from the Holy Word,
  He plied their ears, unwilling of the truth,
And when they could not answer, "I have heard
  That ye be asses, now I know 'tis true."
When called to die he said, "Oh, my white hair,
  What honor hath God had in store for thee?

The crown of martyrdom ye soon shall wear;
   An endless bliss is mine; I go to thee."
Then, kneeling down, he prayed unto his God,
   Prayed for his country, and for those who sent
His spirit to that kingdom where all land;
   And bowing down his head to God he went.
The next to die was Harant, full of woe,
   Not at his death, but that the priests would take
His children in their care, when he was low,
   And they their father's faith must needs forsake.
Perhaps the saddest sight was to behold
   Poor Kaplíř, with his crutches, go to death;
And in a touching story we are told
   How the old man prepared himself for death.
The pastor, Rosacius, who scorned to live,
   And see his brethren die, tells how he went,
And found him in his cell prepared to give
   With radiant joy his body old and bent.
" Long I have prayed the Lord," the old man said,
   " To take me from this world of sorrow sore.
And lo! He heard me not, I must be led
   To feel some pangs our blessed Saviour bore.
It was His will that with my ninety years
   I should go from the scaffold to the throne—
Leave all this misery, all these bitter tears,
   And be at rest forever.   God alone
Knows in my heart I have no sinful thought,
   Nor ever had, 'gainst the dear land I love.
Dear Master, in the faith that you have taught,
   I die, and we shall meet above."
And as he stood, and waited for the call,
   Upon his crutches, with his white head bent
In prayer for the souls that unappalled,
   With fearless faces, to the scaffold went.
They held him out a pardon; " Would he say
   That he had erred, and thereby save his life?"
But sternly the old man said, " Go your way,
   Ye devilish tempters, that but seek out strife.
Heaven breaks upon my view, should earth awake
   One vain regret?   Nay, I am glad to die
A martyr for my land, and my faith's sake;
   Christ will reward me; 'tis to Him I fly."

Then slowly walking to the fatal block,
   The brave old man knelt down upon the floor.
"Oh, Lord, my God, Thou art a very rock,
   In times of trouble. Christ, be thou the door
Through which I enter on the life divine."
   The executioner paused, he could not strike
That bowed white head, although the given sign
   Was given by the judges all alike.
So then a priest came up and said, "My lord,
   In your own way, you have called on your God—
I pray you raise your head on high, my lord,
   One moment more and you are with your God."
Smiling, he raised his head, and it was so.
   Ah, me! ah, me! my heart is sad to think
Of all the fearless souls that were laid low,
   And sometimes as I pausing stand and think,
On the old city square, I seem to see
   The scaffold and the drummers standing round,
And the vast multitude of people like a sea,
   Rising now here, now there, with a dull sound
Of cursing on the scene that they behold,
   And prayers for the ones about to die,
And curses on the soldiers over bold,
   That only laughed to hear the people sigh.
And with a start I wake to see the square,
   Silent and lonely in the midday sun.
No matter, honor be to those who dare
   Die unto God, although their days be done.
For their remembrance, shall like scattered seed,
   Bloom into flowers in some far-off day,
And they with joy unutterable shall lead
   Their followers unto Him who is the way.
And He with gracious voice shall say: "Well done,
   Ye faithful servants, enter in the joy,
That was prepared for you before the sun;
   Enter the peace now that knows no alloy."

KRYSPEK'S GOBLET.

In Kralovice,   two hundred years,*
  The family of Kryspek   sleep.
Within the family vault they lie,
  And none can wake their slumbers deep.
Oh, listen to their banquet dread,
For sure upon this earth 'tis said,
  There never was a sadder meal;
  Come listen to their bitter weal.

When the Bílá Hora battle,
  Spite of all valor had been lost,
And the poor Bohemian country
  Had to give itself up for lost,
Then the hangman's business flourished,
And the ground with blood was nourished;
  From the battle now lost for aye,
  Came Kryspek's men, one sad day.

Long before the war now raging,
  Jitka's beauty had minstrels sung.
Every virtue had the maiden,
  And praised she was by every tongue.
Seventeen summers had she wandered
In the castle hall, and pondered,
  While the striplings from far and wide,
  In useless longing for her sighed.

From far and wide they came to woo—
  The Castle Kačerov was sought
By noblest youths, who wished to wed
  The beauteous maiden, so well taught.

*Note.—The bodies of the Kryspek family, for some reason
or other were embalmed; one can see them in the castle in
Kralovice.

But only one, a noble youth—
Boreš, whose words were words of truth,
  Found favor in the maiden's sight;
  He was a brave and goodly knight.

The marriage day was fixed and came—
  It should have been their wedding eve,
When all at once the trumpet's sound
  Called on the warrior youths to leave '
These pleasures, and to go to war—
The enemy was at the door.
  Brave Boreš, with his soldiers few,
  Joined Šlik, and Budoec " The True."

The enemy was stronger far—
  The poor Bohemians lost the day;
Their homes were sacked, their lives were lost,
  The noblest did the conquerors slay.
But midst it all the Kryspek race,
Lived all forgotten on their place;
  They even dared to dream that they
  Were stricken from the list away.

For vengeance with a bloody sword
  Struck down the noblest of the land;
And as the blow fell not, they thought
  They had been pardoned out of hand.
One evening as the Vesper rang,
Passed through the gate, with marshal clang
  The noble Boreš, wild to see
  His Jitka, wife that was to be.

" To-morrow "—went from lip to lip—
  " To-morrow is the wedding day;
To-morrow—let us hope no storm
  Of grief, or sorrow, dim the day."
All things were ready for the feast,
To-morrow they would fetch the priest.
  Well pleased they sat them down to sup,
  By generous cheer and brimming cup.

The clock struck ten, they were about
  To drink the bride and bridegroom's health;
They wished them joy and a long life—
  They wished them happiness and wealth,
When suddenly a trumpet's call,
From herald sent, fell like a pall,
  And changed their mirth to silence dread.
" The herald seeks my lord," was said.

With strange misgiving went the lord,
  To meet the stranger in the hall;
All joy from out his heart had fled,
  He dreaded news that would appall.
But when he saw the herald's face,
And heard the doom against his race,
  He knew that all his fears were true,
  The conqueror's heart no mercy knew.

Pale like a corpse, he back returned—
  Like one who from the grave comes back—
And slowly said, with choking voice:
" Our brothers died upon the rack!
The hour of Kryspek doom is near—
Our glory faded—life made drear.
  Our mildest punishment, to roam,
  Outcasts from country, and from home."

Then bidding all the servants leave
  The room, until the dawn of day,
That not a soul should enter in,
  Nor rouse their slumber till the day.
" For if we want you, we will ring;
  Yea, in the morning, we will ring."
  And when the servants left the hall,
  He shut the door, and spake to all:

" What is to lose, when land is lost?
  Who loses honor, loseth life.
What joy shall then my grandchild know,
  In poverty and daily strife?
If such a desperate fate is ours,
To languish but a few more hours—
  To see our country die, and then
  To die, nay, let us now be men.

" Here, where my childhood's days were spent;
   Here, where my father's bones were laid;
Where I in manhood's strength have lived,
   And wed your mother, beauteous maid;
Where you were born, my children dear;
And loved, and honored, far and near,
   We must forsake, and wander far
   In banishment, oh evil star!

" Our mildest punishment to roam—
   Made beggars in an evil time,
Banished from everything we love—
   Made butts for every idle rhyme."
Then dropping poison in his glass,
He smiling drank, and said, " Alas,
   That I should ask, ' Who goes to death?'"
" We all," they answered with one breath.

" We all," they answered with one breath.
   And merrily the goblet went;
From hand to hand they passed it on,
   And thirteen drank as on it went.
Father and mother, child and youth,
The bride, and bridegroom, all, forsooth,
   Drank gladly of the deadly wine.
   They praised the cup, they praised the wine.

Twelve o'clock struck; they heard the bell
   Call out to prayer in the night;
They prayed to God in prayers low,
   To help them in the deadly fight.
One whispered, then his voice was still.
Another fell, against his will,
   But seven lived—the light burnt low,
   Then out it went—they all lay low.

So Kryspek and his family died,
   United in a common death;
The bride and bridegroom, hand in hand,
   Sat by each other cold in death.
Hand clasped in hand, around the board,
They found them, but their souls had soared
   Beyond their tyrant's little night,
   Into the everlasting light.

DALIBOR.

A Bohemian legend of the fifteenth century.

" What is the meaning of this haste,
    And stir, within the castle gate?
What means these servants, standing pale,
    These men-at-arms that silent wait?
And wherefore are these faggots piled,
    To burn a sinner, or a saint?
Think you we have forgotten Huss—
    Dream you Bohemian hearts are faint?

" Look, look, upon the winding road
    Come men-at-arms in goodly tale;
And down the mountain side they come,
    Come streaming in from every vale.
What is the meaning of all this,
    And wherefore are we called this day?
Lord Dalibor, our mighty lord,
    It seems, has something new to say.

" For whom these faggots? Say perchance,
    To burn our Huss' judges on?
Ah, that would be a royal day—
    Pile on, you fellows, quick, pile on."
" Hush! hush!" the heralds trumpet loud,
    " Our lord stands on the castle wall;
A nobler lord was never born,
    Shout loud, you fellows by the wall."

And when at length a silence fell,
    The noble lord stood forth and spake:
" Bring now the family records old,
    And all the things that pride awake;

Bring forth the quarterings, painted fine,
　The emblems of my noble race,
And throw them on that burning pile;
　There let them burn before my face."

Silent he stood, with sad, stern face,
　And watched the flames that rose on high.
" Here I lay low all worldly pride,
　I longing but for my land to die.
Is any here that I have wronged,
　Or burdened in my lordly right,
I beg him to forgive me now—
　Let me go blameless in the fight."

The multitude in silence stood;
　They watched the mighty flames rise high.
Then all at once their lord's voice said:
" Oh, brothers mine, now let us die;
Come, let us die for this our land,
　Down-trodden 'neath the German yoke;
Come, let us die for this our faith."
　Shouts drown his voice as thus he spoke.

" No earthly flag, but this the Chalice,
　Shall lead us on, in battle's roar;
I am no noble, but a friend
　Whose right it is to go before.
Take horses, weapons, to your fill—
　Come, let us march against the foe.
Long live Bohemia, our dear land,
　God's praise we'll sing as forth we go."

At these brave words a deaf'ning shout
　Came from that multitude of men:
" Long live our brother Dalibor,
　The leader of Bohemian men."
And soon they were upon the plain,
　And fearless met the angry foe.
God gave the victory to their hands;
　Their enemies were stricken low.

The banner with the Chalice cup
　Was crowned with many a laurel bough,
And day by day their numbers grew.
　The Lord of battles, He knows how

That the Bohemian nation rose,
  Without a fear, to do His will;
They were content for Him to die,
  And for their land their blood to spill.

The royalists were beaten hard;
  They fled before the Hussite band.
Once more one heard the Hussite song
  Resound through the Bohemian land.
One morning in the distant west
  A warrior came, of features cold;
He begged to be allowed to fight;
  He said he was a warrior bold.

He spake they " were a godless set,"
  Those royalists from where he came,
And offered to show Dalibor
  A way to victory, and to fame.
They were to steal away at night
  Along a path that he would show;
Thus easily the royal band
  They could strike down with one quick blow.

Alas! alas! that Dalibor
  Did listen to that lying tongue;
Ah me! he led them all to death,
  And dungeon cell, as bards have sung;
And Dalibor was led in chains,
  And shut in Hradčan's dismal tower.
Oft by the loophole he would sit,
  Unconscious of the passing hour.

One day he said, " Oh, jailer mine,
  Thou seest I will soon be dead;
I pray thee by thy father's ghost,
  I pray thee by thy blessed dead;
Oh, give me but a violin,
  That I may ease my breaking heart.
It cannot harm thee, jailer mine,
  And it will soothe my bitter part."

The jailer was a kindly man,
  He let the prisoner have his way;
And all night long, poor Dalibor
  Upon his instrument did play.

'Tis said, he played with wondrous skill;
   From far and wide the people came;
They used to stand by Hradčan's walls,
   And speak of Dalibor and fame.

They listened, and they wept aloud;
   They listened, and their blood would boil;
For in that simple song they heard
   The anthem of their native soil.
The mountains caught it wailing back,
   A song so strange, they shuddering heard;
The river took it, bore it back,
   With a strange murmur that allured.

Each day the crowd became more dense,
   To listen to that music wild;
They spake of country, and of God—
   They said the man was good and mild.
One day King Ladislav rode by;
   He eyed them with a cruel look,
And when at length the cause he knew,
   With rage and wrath he fairly shook.

He ordered that the violin
   Should broken be on dungeon wall,
And laughingly he went next day,
   And sneering said, " What can befall?"
But lo! beneath dark Hradčan's wall
   The people stand, and listening hear
The anthem of their native land,
   Played by a hand that knows no fear.

Then, white with rage, the king said, " Kill
   The man that dares to play that lay."
And soon the bloody head was seen—
   But still the hand unseen did play.
The people, with a shuddering dread,
   Knocked down the guards, and onward rushed;
They only found the broken wood—
   The body, from which the blood gushed.

But still the hand unseen doth play.
The anthem of their native land.
And even now by Hradčan's walls,
Some say, that still a magic hand
Is heard to play, when patriots high
Beneath the ramparts sadly stray.
'Tis said, that those who once have heard
Can ne'er forget that haunting lay.

THE ENCHANTED MAID.

A Bohemian legend of the fifteenth century.

The forest leaves were bright and green,
  And soft the zephyr blew.
The mountain peaks were lost to view,
  In clouds of pearly gray.
With happy steps two Checkish boys
Went singing of their many joys,
  As through the wood they went.
They might have been two happy guests
  Upon a wedding bent.

They sang of love, they sang of woe,
  With voices high and sweet;
And oft they sang, that life is fleet,
  And love as strong as death.
At length the eldest one said, "Wait!
Here is a splendid tree that fate
  Has thrown into our way.
We'll cut it down and make ourselves
  Two harps this sunny day."

They set about to cut that tree,
  With boyish laughter wild.
And oft they sang, and oft they smiled,
  As happily they plied.
But when they reached the inmost heart,
They both fell back as though a dart
  Had struck their own young life,
For there a beauteous maiden stood
  And begged of them her life.

But even as the maiden spoke,
  She shivered and turned pale,
And then she sank with a great wail
  Upon the emerald grass.
" 'Tis not your fault, oh, happy boys,
So full of life and earthly joys,
  That takes me from this earth.
My mother did enchant me so
  To keep me from all mirth.

" I had a lover fair like you,
  And often did we meet,
Ah, me! the hours passed so fleet,
  And we were very young.
My mother, with her evil eye,
She soon found out the reason why
  I would not do her will,
And gather 'neath the moon's bright beam
  The plants that work out ill.

" And so, she turned me to a tree,
  While I stood with my love.
I pray you, youths, by Him above,
  To grant me but one boon—
Make harps from out this fallen tree,
And go and tell the world of me—
  And for my mother play.
Oh, play and sing of all my woe,
  That she may rue her day."

And so she died, that maiden fair,
  Upon the emerald grass;
And the two youths took up the lass,
  And laid her in the sod.
Then sadly they obeyed her will,
And made them harps with Checkish skill,
  To touch her mother's heart.
Ah, melancholy was the wail
  Of their new-fashioned harp.

Before her mother's house they stopped,
  And struck a solemn strain.
It almost seemed a soul in pain,
  That sang from out their harps:
" Oh, brave young men, I bid you go—
Your song, it is too full of woe,
  Like some poor soul in pain;
And still it strikes me that I know
  That tearful song again."

The youths, they would not leave her side;
  They played with wilder skill;
They sang, " Oh, mother, take thy fill
  Of malediction now."
And never from her human ears
Was hushed that song so full of fears
  Until she dying lay.
And I have heard that devils came
  And took her soul away.

THE BRIDE OF HEAVEN.

A BOHEMIAN BALLAD.

" When I used to go and see thee,
  Stand beneath thy window sill,
See, I was quite sure, beloved one,
  That we were one heart, one will.
Never did I think, beloved one,
  We must part, I loving still.

"And the last time that I saw thee
  Weaving a fair myrtle wreath,
I sat watching, never thinking
  Why you did not bind the leaf.
Now I pray thee, loved one, tell me,
  Why unfinished is the wreath?

"I was thinking, thinking sadly—
  Thinking as I think to-day,
That we cannot wed, beloved one,
  That our farewell we must say;
So I left the wreath unfinished,
  Left unfinished to this day.

" They would force me to be married
  To a youth I cannot love;
They would drag me to the altar,
  Sacrifice me like a dove;
They would force me to be wedded
  To a lad I cannot love.

" They would force me to be married,
  Though I loath his very sight.
Go get ready for the wedding—
  It will be a merry sight.
Go prepare the wedding banquet,
  While I dress my hair aright.

" Yes, they shall prepare the wedding,
    In the convent far away.
Come, oh bridesmaids, cut my long locks,
    Let me sup with you to-day.
Gladly in your silent convent,
    I will give my hand away.

" Come and see me, oh beloved—
    Come and hear me when I sing,
Till that fatal day, beloved,
    When the black robe they will fling
Round about my weary shoulders—
    On my hand the wedding ring.

" They will take my white dress from me,
    Dress me in the robe of pain;
And the image of my bridegroom
    Now must be my only gain.
Vanish from my sight, beloved one,
    We must never meet again.

" The crucifix is by my side,
    The rosary in my hand,
I raise my weary eyes to Him,
    Lord of that heavenly band.
Oh, glorious bridegroom, I am yours,
    The wedding ring is on my hand.

" Beyond the convent's silent walls,
    Oh, never more shall I stray,
No earthly voice shall haunt me more,
    When I humbly kneel to pray.
Heaven's love will fill my broken heart,
    The world will have passed away.

"Avaunt from me, beloved of earth,
    My bridegroom is in the sky;
Depart from me, betrothed on earth,
    To Heaven I fain would fly;
Oh, holy bridegroom, fill my heart
    With your image till I die.

" Oh, vain indeed, the love of earth,
    To still my poor heart's aching.
Come to me, oh, thou crucified,
    And keep my heart from breaking;
Oh, take me, Lord, unto Thyself,
    I, my vain life forsaking."

She knelt before the crucifix,
    She called on her lover high.
" Oh, loved of God, oh, bridegroom mine,
    Be my defense till I die.
My faint heart yearns to see thy face,
    And thy glory up on high."

The heavenly bridegroom heard her voice,
    He knew her heart was broken.
He said, " Thy prayer is heard, my bride,
    This is the promised token."
A rapture came within her heart—
    Men said she died heartbroken.

JOHN, SACRIFICED JOHN.

AN OLD BOHEMIAN LEGEND.

Gather round me, little laddies,
  And ye maidens small;
Listen to my voice and lyre;
  Listen, children all.
With attention hear my ballad,
  Till the tale be done;
Listen—'tis a wondrous story—
  Till my song be done.

In a poor Bohemian village,
  Not far from the way,
Even now you see an old well,
  Honored till this day.
Deep within it lies a church bell,
  Hid from mortal eyes;
Never more its voice shall ringing
  Bid us praise the skies.

Only once in the far ages
  Did they hear its voice,
When an old religious woman
  Went there once by choice.
Dipping in its cold, clear bosom
  Linen she had spun,
Half drew up the bell that lay there,
  Hid from light and sun.

Filled with horror, she fell fainting
  By the old well's side,
And her weak hands left their holding,
  And the bell did slide,

With a terrible resounding,
  That shook hill and dale,
Back into the old well's darkness,
  While its voice did wail:
" John, John, sacrificed John."

PART SECOND.

With a dark scowl on his forehead,
  Homeward rides the Checkish lord.
By his side, the staghounds leading,
  Follows John, page to my lord.
Like a thundercloud his forehead,
  And his eyes with anger burn;
For his dearest dog is missing,
  And he knows not where to turn.

Three whole days they have been searching
  Wood, and field, and everywhere.
Useless is their toil and seeking,
  And their looking everywhere.
Sadly, with their faces troubled,
  Back they turn them to their home,
While their lord with bosom swelling,
  Sighs, " My dog, where do you roam?"

On the road there stands a granny,
  Leaning on her crutches two.
See! her head is like an owl's head,
  And she has but one eye, too;
Humpbacked, all her face a wrinkle—
  And her hands but skin and bone;
Voice—why like a rook in cawing
  Is the harsh and gutteral tone.

" Stop your charger! Stop your people!
  Listen to my words, I say.
Wherefore do you search the forests
  And the meadows all the day?
I can tell you of your staghound,
  Of the fleet one that you love,
But I must be paid to do it;
  I am seeking gain—not love.

" If you give me your page, Johnny,
      Hound is yours, to-morrow morn.
Why I want him? Oh, a witch knows,
      Human blood makes flesh newborn.
In the stars I see it written,
      Johnny's blood can make me young.
Human blood can make old woman
      Once more beautiful and young."

At these words the wretched stripling
      Felt his heart turn to a stone.
Between fears and hopes he trembles,
      Kneels upon the grass alone.
" Mercy, mercy, O loved master;
      Listen to my voice, I pray,
And the life of a true servant,
      Give not for a dog away."

But his master, only heeding
      The strong voice within his heart,
Not the pale and tear-stained features,
      Hardened unto him his heart.
" Bring the staghound—bring him, granny,
      When the day begins to break.
By my faith—without a question—
      Then my Johnny you can take."

PART THIRD.

When the day dawned, at the gateway
      Stood the foul witch, with the hound.
And Johnny, looking from the casement,
      Saw his death, and not the hound.
" Mercy, mercy, oh my master!
      Show me mercy—let me live—
Give me not to the foul sorceress;
      Let me see the sun and live."

But his master, in his rapture,
      Deaf is to the stripling's voice.
Witch and dog he clasps together—
      Orders then a banquet choice.

When the evening shadows lengthen,
  Bound with chains they bring the youth.
In a car, with dragon horses,
  Lost is witch and youth, forsooth.

PART FOURTH.

Hardly five weeks was the staghound
  Once more with his lord,
When the dearly bought one sickened,
  Died before his lord;
Then his master, in a frenzy,
  . Tore his hair in woe.
But the dog lay dead for all that—
  John was lying low.

When at length his pain was duller,
  And some days had passed,
Human feeling woke within him,
  And he felt at last
What a sin he had committed
  When he gave the lad
To the witch; and lone and haunted,
  Sat he still and sad.

" Johnny—poor devoted Johnny,"
  Often did he say,
" To a fearful death I gave you,
  On an evil day.
Oh, nod to me from thy heaven,
  That I am forgiven.
Oh, show mercy to me, Johnny,
  Say I am forgiven."

After that he built a chapel,
  Not far from the well;
And a wooden tower also,
  With a silver bell—
With a bell of purest silver
  They were bid to toll -
Every day, in rain and sunshine,
  For poor Johnny's soul.

When they first began their tolling
  For the poor lad's soul,
Back they started in wild horror,
  Says the legend old.
For it was no bell of silver,
  But a human cry,
Echoing in their ears bewildered, ·
  Like a human sigh:
" John, John, sacrificed John."

PART FIFTH.

And the lord of Kozojedy
  Hearing, turned to stone.
Then he tore his rich robes from him,
  While his heart did groan.
" Bring me now the hair-cloth garments
  Of a penitent;
I shall be from henceforth ringer,
  Till my life be spent."

Strange to say, the bitter anguish,
  And the endless pain,
That had made his life a burden,
  Passed away like rain;
And the bell rang out in gladness,
  In the morning air:
Rang out like a seraph singing
  In the trembling air.

Once, long after from the ringing,
  Never home came he;
But they found him by the tower,
  From his penance free.
On his face a heavenly rapture
  To the world did say,
That his sins, however dreadful,
  Had been done away.

PART SIXTH.

Years passed by, war with its horrors
  Broke o'er the Bohemian land.
Down went chapel, down went tower,
  Leveled by the robber band.

Yes, the silver bell they wanted;
   But God's will was greater still;
Angel hands were sent to guard it,
   In the well it lingered still.

Deep it lies amidst the waters
   And the pebbles of the well;
All around it life is stirring,
   As the hunter's horn can tell.
But the bell was bound to silence,
   Till the hour of fate drew near,
And the weak hand of a woman
   Pulled it up without a fear.

Only halfway could she pull it,
   But the voice rang, clear and long:
" John, John, John, sacrificed John!"
   Ah, never more shall that song
Be heard of a mortal again,
   Though many come to the well
To water their linen again.
   Though many the story tell,
None can say they have heard its voice,
   For the bell is hid in the well,
Never more to be heard on earth.

THE STORY OF A LOST SOUL.

A BOHEMIAN LEGEND.

Across a verdant meadow,
   Whose diamond dews were tears,
Two blessed souls were walking;
   They had not any fears;
And just behind them, sighing,
   Came a lost soul in tears.

At length they reached the gateway,
   And knocking at the door,
Stood praying at the threshold
   To Him whose name they bore;
With radiant faces waiting,
   The opening of that door.

Our Lord said to St. Peter,
   " Who knocks, I pray thee see."
" Two blessed souls, my Saviour,
   Who long thy face to see;
And a very sinful soul,
   Who fain to Thee would flee."

The Lord said, " Let them enter,
   Those righteous souls and true;
But show that sinful soul
   The road that leads to rue;
Where she in cleansing fire,
   Shall mourn her sins, not few."

That poor soul went lamenting,
  And weeping very sore,
Till tears of blood were sprinkled,
  Upon the robe she wore.
And still her gaze kept seeking,
  That distant, close-shut door.

And while she wandered sadly,
  And thought upon her dole,
She saw the blessed Virgin,
  Who gazed upon her soul,
And asked in accents tender,
  " Poor soul, what is thy dole?"

" Alas! alas! " she answered,
  " My sins are very great,
I cannot enter Heaven,
  My soul in Hell must wait.
Alas! alas! dear mother,
  Have pity on my fate."

The Blessed Virgin answered,
  " I can do nought but pray,
Come with me, erring daughter,
  Upon this narrow way.
And when we come to Heaven,
  I for thy soul will pray."

With trembling fear and anguish—
  With many, many tears,
The poor soul stood and waited,
  And struggled with her fears,
While the loud knock resounded,
  And thundered in her ears.

Our Lord said to St. Peter,
  " Go see who knocketh so?"
" My Lord, it is your Mother,
  With a lost soul from woe."
" Then let my mother enter,
  But the sinful soul must go."

" Not so, not so, beloved,
    My son, I pray thee hear,
Have mercy, I beseech thee,
    Upon this soul in fear.
And turn her bitter anguish
    To songs of praise, just here."

" Right gladly would I hear thee,
    Oh, Blessed Mother mine,
But in my Father's mansions
    That sinful soul would pine;
What good work has she finished,
    Meet for this home divine?"

" Alas! alas! I sinful
    Have walked in my own light;
The world and all its pleasures,
    They were my sole delight;
Alas! I am most sinful,
    Most sinful in my sight."

" But say, some good work surely—
    Some fasts you must have kept?"
The Blessed Mother questioned,
    The sinful soul that wept:
" Some sins you must have thought of,
    And prayed for, ere you slept?"

" Alas! alas! I sinful
    Have nothing I can show,
Except I sometimes tended
    The sick ones in their woe,
And gave a little water
    To those down-stricken low."

Ah, great then was the beauty,
    That shown in our Lord's face:
" Give me thy hand, redeemed one,
    Thy sins they are effaced;
Come in, come in, redeemed one,
    Thou, too, hast won the race."

And by the hand He took her,
    And led her to the throne.
" This one," He said, " did drink me,
    And tend me when alone.
This act, oh Holy Father,
    For all her sins atone."

THE DEVIL'S BRIDE.

A BOHEMIAN BALLAD.

There was a virtuous lady,
  Who had daughters three to marry;
With two of them she went to church,
  For the third she would not tarry.
The girl laughed loud, and dressed her hair,
  For she had a mind to marry.

She thought in our little garden
  There are plenty of roses fair;
I will make them into a wreath;
  A beautiful wreath, I will wear.
Said a tall young man, passing by,
  " Maid, give me the wreath from your hair."

" The wreath's not for you, tall young man,
  I wait for a nobler than you."
And she wandered amidst the flowers,
  The roses of many hue.
Said a bold young man, passing by,
  " Maid, give me the wreath from your hair."

" The wreath's not for you, bold young man,
  I wait for a nobler than you."
And she smiled a wicked wee smile,
  A smile that to her was not new.
Said a dark young man, riding by,
  " Maid, give me the wreath from your hair."

" I'll give you the wreath from my hair,
   For a nobler I will not wait."
Then the dark young man stopped his steed,
   And the vain girl mounted elate,
While he whisp ered low in her ears,
" I'll take thee to paradise straight."

And away they rode through the town,
   Till they came to an awful way;
There were stunted and blasted trees;
   There were snakes there ready to slay,
And there many a poison herb
   Grew, that hid from the light of day.

And far away in the distance
   The vain girl saw the flames of hell,
That leaped with their tongues of fire
   'Gainst the sky they hated so well.
And their steed rushed on like the wind,
   And soon they were standing in hell.

" Open, my comrades, my black ones,
   I have brought you a vain young girl."
The door flew open, and devils,
   Yea, hundreds flew out with a whirl.
And they danced and capered with glee,
   And they laughed at the vain young girl.

" Where are your manners, you devils?
   Bring the lady a glass of wine."
Then one of the devils ran quick,
   And soon brought her a goblet fine.
" Drink, thou vainest of maidens, drink,
   The health of our prince in this wine."

She drank of that wine and turned pale;
   She drank, and flames rushed from her lips.
" Oh, prince of this country," she said,
   " Oh, moisten with water my lips."
The devils laughed loud at her call,
   They said, "'Take long draughts, make no sips."

" Let me breathe air but a moment—
 A moment in pity, I pray."
But the devils, laughing, replied,
" That is easy enough to say;
Had you but lived a better life,
 You would not have been here to-day."

The girl wept aloud in despair:
" My soul I have lost now for aye,
Oh, would I could tell my mother,
 To teach my poor sisters to pray;
Oh, would I could go to the earth,
 I would turn them from sin away."

" Cease from thy fretting and worrying,
 There are plenty to teach the way.
If the sisters choose to listen
 They can also learn how to pray.
You chose to do ill in your life,
 And your soul is lost now for aye."

THE LOVER BY THE GRAVE.

A BOHEMIAN BALLAD.

Passing through the somber forest,
    Maidens two I saw.
" Tell me, maidens, tell me, fair ones,
    That I hold in awe,
Is my loved one midst your number,
Making hay, or doth she slumber?"

" Ah, alas! your loved one slumbers,
    Deep within the grave.
Yesterday we laid her lowly,
    Where the grasses wave."
" Dead! my loved one, oh, tell me where
Lies my loved one, without compare?"

" 'Tis a fair way that we took her,
    Winding up the hill;
Where the youths trod there are pebbles,
    You can see them still.
Where the maidens trod are roses,
There she lies in death's encloses."

" Tell me, maidens, where she sleepeth,
    Whom I loved so well."
" Not far from the gateway, lover,
    By the graveyard cell."
Twice I wandered round God's acre,
Praying sore unto my Maker.

Weeping midst the graves I sought her,
    Who had been my bride;
But her lowly grave I found not,
    Though I wept and sighed.
" Who disturbs our peaceful sleeping? "
Said a voice, as I stood weeping.

" Oh, beloved one, break thy slumber,
    Come from out thy grave;
Three years I have yearned to see thee
    And I find thy grave!"
" But my heart is cold within me,
I am dead, and cannot love thee.

" Look around and find a shovel,
    Make me free from earth;
Take me home, then, my beloved one,
    'Midst the bridal mirth."
I dug deep, I found my loved one,
Cold and pale I found my loved one.

In her wedding dress I saw her,
    With the myrtle wreath;
But her eyes were closed in slumber,
    She had drank of lethe.
" Take the ring off from my finger—
Wherefor, lover, dost thou linger?

" Throw the ring into the river,
    It will bring thee peace;
Leave me, then, in peaceful sleeping,
    Let thy sorrow cease.
For my heart is cold within me,
I am dead, and cannot love thee."

" Oh, ring ye church bells, far and wide,
    That my bride is dead,
Then ring ye church bells, long and loud,
    That my heart is dead.
Oh, lay me in the self-same grave
With her whom I had died to save."

THE WIZARD.

A BOHEMIAN LEGEND.

Through the dark and lonely forest,
  Sparingly the sunlight fell;
Round the forests, rocky mountains,
  Where the eagle's brood doth dwell;
By a little stream of water,
  In a cave amidst the rocks,
Dwelt the wizard of Podjokly,
  Old and bent, with snowy locks.

Far and wide they came to see him,
  Asking help, and begging aid;
And 'twas said he could do wonders—
  But he must be richly paid.
When the shades of evening gather,
  Like a dark cloud in the sky,
Once there came a muffled figure,
  Hid from every prying eye.

" Wizard, can your magic tell me,
  What his fate was who wore this?
Name your price, but tell me truly,
  Is your knowledge up to this? "
In his hand he placed a locket
  With a curl of golden hair.
" Name your price—but tell me truly,
  Where is he who owned this hair? "

Then the wizard lit his fire—
  Took his hood and drew his spell.
Then he said, " The youth's voice whispers
  From the ground where he doth dwell.

Listen—do you hear the whisper—
  He was killed by murder foul!
And his murderer hid the body
  Near a cave where foxes howl."

" Wizard, can you say who killed him—
  He who was my lord on earth?
Name your price, but tell me truly,
  Does he still live on the earth?"
Then the wizard rose up stately,
  And said slow, "Accursed one!
Do you doubt my magic power—
  You are that accursed one!"

" Yes, you killed your stripling nephew,
  To inherit his broad land;
And you come here but to question
  If detection is at hand.
Do you dream to cheat a wizard,
  As you cheated that poor lad?
Yes, detection dogs your footsteps,
  You shall see the murdered lad.

" Never from this forest's shadow
  Shall you wander out again;
Even now they bring his body;
  With your dagger he was slain."
At these words the muffled stranger,
  With a shriek rushed to the door,
But he fell back, swooning, fainting,
  At the burden that they bore.

Half devoured by the foxes,
  Lay the lord of vast estate;
On his knees a raving madman,
  Laughed his uncle o'er his fate.
Through the dark and somber forest,
  Home they bore the murdered youth;
But his uncle left that forest,
  Nevermore on earth, forsooth.

THREE AGES IN BOHEMIA.

PART FIRST.

There was a time when the Bohemian land
    Was known and honored, throughout the wide world's
      length,
For mighty warriors and heroic men
    Her name was honored, bravery was her strength.

There was an age when every one was proud
    To call himself a son of that fair land,
Where every art was known and learning prized;
    And praise was given to the skillful hand.

There was an age when the Bohemian tongue
    Was spoken from the throne in accents clear;
Divinest harmony, their native speech,
    In palace homes was spoken far and near.

That time, Bohemian men were proud to say
    They were Bohemians, sons of that brave land,
Where the dread lion was their coat-of-arms,
    And wealth and plenty smiled upon the land.

PART SECOND.

Then the times changed, misfortune came apace,
    And they forgot that which they once had been.
Indifference, lethargy, upon them crept,
    They thought no more, they lived as in a dream.

Bohemian hearts grew cold, their native land
    They loved no more, forgotten was their pride—
Forgotten were the deeds their fathers did—
    They were not worthy to sleep by their side.

Then they denied their land, their blood, their speech—
   Their father's cherished things, from them they cast.
And took upon them foreign ways and speech,
   Forgetting their land's brothers of the past.

Then the Bohemian sun grew dark and dim,
   And its good genius stood and wept afar.
Their poets praised no more their native land,
   Their muse was dead—had fled afar, afar.

What thoughts were his who stood and saw all this!
   Remembering the great past and mighty dead?
He whose heart beat but for his native land—
   To see her lying there before him dead.

PART THIRD.

But hark! Arise! The angel of the Lord
   Sounds from his trumpet, "Come from out thy
      grave.
Arise! awake! and from thy every church
   Let national songs be sung thy land to save."

Thus spake the angel, and the love of land
   Woke up a thousand shades from out their graves.
The dying heard it, and awoke again,
   Praising the Lord that they no more were slaves.

The spirit of their fathers came again,
   Imbuing with new life their torpid hearts.
Gladly they heard the call. Awake! arise!
   Sing praises in your churches and your marts.

Awake! arise! all ye that slumber still!
   The day is dawning—see the light breaks through.
The nightingales are singing—wherefore sleep?
   Shame to the sluggards—let them be but few.

Oh brothers, live again but for your land—
   Be ye not dead unto her urgent need.
Oh, be ye brothers, be ye sons again,
   Unto your native land in her great need,

Reverence your laws, your customs, and your rights,
  Show in your lives you are Bohemians true;
Then shall our land once more be known to fame,
  As in the ancient times when ye were true.

DEDICATED

THE WEDDING SHIRT.

The eleventh hour was past and gone,
But still the lamp burnt on and on.

The lamp that on the praying chair
Cast an uneven, ghastly glare.

On the low wall a picture hung,
God's parents, praised by every tongue.

The parents with the Holy Child,
Roses, with rosebud, saintly mild.

Before the heavenly three a maid
Upon her knees her prayers said.

Her face shone with a holy rest,
Her arms were crossed upon her breast.

And as her tears fell soft and slow,
Her bosom swelled with hidden woe.

Her tears they fell like diamonds bright
Upon her bosom snowy white.

" Alas, my God! my father lies
Beneath the grass, dust in his eyes.

" Alas, my God! my mother sleeps
Beside him—there where no one weeps.

" My sister died within a year;
In battle fell my brother dear.

" But though so lonely, still I loved
　Above myself a youth beloved.

" He wandered far to earn his bread—
　And came no more—perhaps is dead.

" Before he went away he said,
　Wiping my tears, ' We soon shall wed.'

" ' Sow flax, my loved one, in your field;
　God give you have a bounteous yield.

" ' The first year spin the flaxen thread,
　Then bleach it white, we soon shall wed;
　The third year, sew thy shirt,' he said.

" ' And when the shirt is sewed, my fair,
　Then make a garland for thy hair.'

" The shirt I finished, put away,
　And there it lies unto this day.

" My wreath is faded, withered now—
　But where art thou? Oh, where art thou?

" In the wide world you went away,
　Wide as the sea, I heard them say.

" Three years have passed—I do not know
　If still you live—perhaps lie low.

" Mary! Virgin of mighty strength!
　Give me, give me thy aid at length.

" Bring, oh, bring, my loved again—
　Make an end of my lingering pain.

" Bring my loved to me again,
　Or let me die—my life is vain.

" I hoped indeed to be his wife—
　And without him—well, what is life!

" Mary! Mother of Mercy, hear,
And grant my prayer even here."

The pictured face bowed low her head—
The maiden shrieked, and would have fled.

The lamp that had been burning dim
Went out.   Was it the north-wind's whim?

" Was it the wind—or can it be
Some evil token unto me?

" Hush! Did I hear a timid tap
Upon the window, rap, rap, rap."

" Art thou asleep, or dost thou wake?
Up, my beloved! Up, for my sake.

" Up, my beloved, and look at me—
If you still know me, I would see.
And is thy hand and heart still free?"

" Oh! my beloved, and can it be!
See I was thinking just of thee.

" Praying indeed that we might meet,
That God might lead thy wandering feet."

" Leave thy praying, and come with me—
Bah on thy praying—come with me!

" The moon is shining far and wide,
Come quick with me, come quick, my bride."

" For God's sake! Why, my love, 'tis night—
'Tis late—wait only for the light.

" The wind howls, and the night is dark,
Wait till the dawn, and then we start."

" Bah! Day is night and night is day—
I dream in the daytime—come away.

" Before the cock crows, thou must be
My wife, so come along with me.

" Don't talk, but come along with me,
Ere the day dawn, my wife thou'lt be."

It was deep midnight when they went,
The moon far off watched, nearly spent.

The landscape lay in silence deep,
Only the wind it would not sleep.

And he went onward, striding fast,
She, step for step, behind him passed.

The dogs came out and howled in choir,
When'er they passed a cottage door.

And see, they saw a strange, strange sight,
A corpse that walked about at night.

" The night is fine—such nights the dead
Rise from their graves, I've heard it said.

" And ere one knows, stand by one's side—
My love doth fear? Wouldst thou hide?"

" Why should I fear? Why should I hide?
God is above—thou by my side.

" But tell me, is your father well?
And will he like with me to dwell?

" And is your mother satisfied,
To have me always by her side?"

" Why, my beloved one, do you ask?
Keep your health only for this task.

" To reach our home—come quick, come quick—
The way is long—thou art not quick.

" What hast thou in thy hand, my bride?"
" My mass book, that no ill betide."

" Throw it away, 'tis like a stone—
  I hate to hear thy praying tone.

" Throw it away, thou'll lighter be,
  Throw it away, and come with me."

He took the book, and tossed away—
They gained ten miles upon the way.

And the path was rocky and lone,
Amidst forests that made a moan.

And behind the mountains and rocks
Howled the wild dogs, in savage flocks.

And the voice of the screech-owl told
Of evil that threatened the bold.

And he went onward, striding fast,
She, step for step, behind him passed.

Across the stony, rocky way,
Her white feet went that evil day.

And e'en the weeds, and tangled grass,
Were stained with blood as she did pass.

" The night is fine—such nights the dead
Walk with the living, I've heard said.

" And ere one knows, stand by one's side—
My love doth fear?   Wouldst thou hide?"

" Why should I fear?   Why should I hide?
God is above—thou by my side.

" But, tell me, is your cottage large?
And who, my love, has it in charge?

" Is the room big? And is it bright?
   Is the church, loved one, within sight?"

" Much, my fair one, you question me;
   Come on, quick, then you soon will see.

" Quicken thy pace, the way is long,
   Time flies, yes, quicker, then a song.

" What hangs about thy waist, I pray?"
" My rosary I took on the way."

" Thy rosary! It winds like a snake—
   It makes me anxious for thy sake.

" Throw it away, it stops thy speed,
   And follow quickly where I lead."

The rosary he threw away—
   Twenty miles they were on their way.

And the road was swampy and bad,
   By morasses, desolate, sad.

O'er the marshes the corpse-lights shone,
   Ghastly blue they glimmered alone.

Nine on each side, they went ahead,
   As though they burned for some poor dead.

The frogs they sang the burial hymn,
   The blue lights flickered and grew dim.

And he went onward, striding fast,
   She wearily behind him passed.

Poor maiden, why your feet are sore,
   And blood runs where your feet you tore.

The weeds are covered with your blood,
   But on he strides with heavy thud.

" The night is fine—such nights the dead
  Seek out the living, I've heard said.

" And ere one thinks, one's grave is near—
  Say, my beloved, dost thou fear? "

" I fear not; thou art by my side—
  And God's will—why it must betide.

" But wait a moment, let me stay,
  And rest a while upon the way."

Her soul was faint, her knees were weak,
And swords seemed in her heart to meet.

" Come quick, come quick, oh maiden mine,
  Our home is near, make no repine.

" The banquet's spread—the guests they wait—
  Time flies, we surely will be late.

" What hast thou on that ribbon fine
  Upon thy throat, oh loved one mine? "
" My mother's cross—the cross divine."

" Ha, ha, that golden cross it pricks—
  I see the blood it slowly tricks.

" It wounds you—cast it from you now,
  Then you'll speed on, you know not how."

The cross he took, and cast away—
Thirty miles they gained on their way.

Upon a wide and open plain
She saw a building once again.

The windows they were narrow, high,
A bell hung in the turret nigh.

" Look, my beloved one, we are near,
  How does it please thee, let me hear? "

" Ah God!   It is a church I see."
" 'Tis no church, but belongs to me!"

" That churchyard, and those crosses thine?"
" No crosses—trees for which I pine!

" Look on me, loved one, over all,
Then quickly jump over the wall."

" Oh, let me be, thy look is wild—
Thou art no longer gentle, mild.

" Thy breath is like a poison rare,
Thy heart it is no longer there."

" Oh, fear me not!   A happy life
Is thine if thou wilt be my wife.

" Meat thou'lt have—without blood I say,
Except by hazard—just to-day.

" What hast thou in thy bundle there?"
" The shirts I made of linen fair."

" Two are enough—throw them away,
One for us each, enough I say."

He threw the bundle on the wall,
It fell upon a gravestone tall.

" Be not afraid, but look at me,
And jump across the wall you see."

" You went before me all the way,
Then lead across the wall, I pray.

" I followed but the path you trod,
Jump over first upon the sod."

He jumped across the churchyard wall,
He thought of treason not at all.

Five feet he leaped into the air,
Then he looked back, no maid was there.

But like a flash he saw a form
Glide by him, in the dark, forlorn.

There stood indeed a chamber small,
One heard the latchstring quickly fall.

A narrow room, with windows none—
Through chinks the moonlight passage won.

And in that cage-like room on bier,
A corpse is laid with no one near.

Ah, what is this—this nameless fear—
The ghouls are stirring—they are here!

One hears them—they are gliding on—
And strange and weird their ghostly song.

" The body to the earth is told,
Alas! for him who lost his soul."

And on the door one heard them rap,
And awful was their tap, tap, tap.

" Arise, oh dead one, from thy bier,
Pull back the latch, we all are here."

The dead one opens wide his eyes,
He makes as though he would arise.

His head he raises from the bier,
He looks about him, far and near.

" Great God! Thy mercy now I pray—
Oh, keep me from the devil's sway!"

" You dead one, lay you down to sleep—
God in His mercy, thy soul keep."

The corpse lay down again in peace,
Of sleep he took another lease.

But listen! Once again the rap,
And stronger now their tap, tap, tap.

" Arise, oh dead one, from thy bier,
Open the room—the dead are here."

And at that knock, and at that song,
The dead woke from his slumbers strong.

He stretched his stiff arm to the door,
And would perhaps have gained the floor.

" Christ save thy soul!   And mercy give—
He can and will, thy sins forgive! "

" You dead one, lay you down to sleep,
God give you joy, and slumber deep."

The corpse he stretched him out again,
And stiffly lay as he had lain.

And once again that awful rap—
Her head reeled as she heard that tap.

" Arise, oh dead one, from thy bier,
Give us the living—do you hear? "

Alas! alas! poor maiden mine,
The dead are here, for the third time.

The dead stares from his sunken eyes,
He looks to where the maiden lies.

" Mary! Mother of God, be near!
Pray to thy son, I fear, I fear!

" The prayer I prayed it was not right,
Forgive me! Save me in thy might.

THE WEDDING SHIRT.

"Mary! Mother of mercy hear!
  Save me, oh save me, even here."

And see—just at that moment dread,
  The cock crows, and the dead falls dead.

And all around the cocks crow clear,
  The night is past, the dawn is near.

The dead one lies upon the floor,
  Just as he went to open the door.

Without the silence is profound,
  Unbroken by a single sound.

The sun rose high, the people came,
  To hear the mass and praise God's name.

A new and open grave they found—
  The girl was in the dead-house round.

A wedding favor on each mound,
  Made from her shirts, they quickly found.

They filled the grave, and burnt with care,
  Each rag that they found anywhere.

The maiden from a foreign part,
  They kindly took unto their heart.

"Well for you, maiden, that you prayed,
  Of evil that you were afraid;
  And even in God's ways have strayed.

"Or, like your shirts, you would have been
  Torn into bits, by ghouls, I ween.

"Well for you that you knelt to pray,
  Or lost your soul had been this day."

THE GOLD SPINNING-WHEEL.

PART FIRST.

A forest and a widening plain—
And see a rider comes amain;
   From out the forest, on fiery steed,
   One hears the horseshoes ring at his speed
     As he rides alone, alone.

And by a hamlet down he sprang,
And on the door knocks, bang, bang, bang.
   " Hola within! come open the door!
   In hunting I've lost my way once more,
     Come, give me water to drink."

Out came a maiden, wondrous fair,
The world n'er saw such beauty rare—
   She brought him water from out the spring,
   Bashfully then, made the spin-wheel sing,
     As she sat there spinning flax.

The rider stops, is looking on,
Forgotten thirst in that sweet song.
   Wondering he watches the fine white thread;
   His eyes are fixed on the bowed fair head
     Of the beautiful spinner.

If your hand is free, maiden mine—
My wife thou'lt be—for thee I pine."
   He fain would have clasped her to his breast,
   But she said, " My mother's will is best,
     And I have no will but hers."

And who may be thy mother, maid?
There's no one here, my maiden staid."
" Oh, sir, my stepmother's in the town,
  She went for her daughter to the town;
    To-morrow they both come home."

PART SECOND.

A forest and a widening plain,
And see the rider comes again
  From out the forest on snowy steed—
  One hears the hoof-irons ring at his speed,
    As he rides to the hamlet.

And by the hamlet down he sprang,
And on the door knocks, bang, bang, bang.
" Hola within, come open the door,
  Let me see thy face, beloved, once more,
    Oh, thou who art my treasure."

Out came a granny, skin and bone:
" Ha! What brings you?" Harsh was her tone
" I bring you a change in house," he said.
" I fain would your handsome daughter wed—
    The one you call not your own."

" Ha! ha! your words are passing strange—
  Who would have thought of such a change!
  Be welcome though, my honorable guest,
  Unknown to me, I still bid you rest—
    Come, tell me how you came here."

" Know I am king of all this land—
  I strayed here from my knightly band.
  I'll give you silver, I'll give you gold
  For that daughter of yours—wealth untold,
    For that beautiful spinner."

" Oh, master king, 'tis strange, most strange—
  Who would have thought of such a change!
  We are not worthy, oh, master king,
  To dare to think of such a thing;
    We are poor, humble people.

" Still one thing—yes, that I can do
For stranger, give my daughter true.
   They are alike—one like the other;
   Like two eyes, from the selfsame mother,
     And see her thread is silken."

" Granny, your words I do not like—
Do as I order, that is right.
   To-morrow when the dawn is nearing,
   Bring your stepdaughter, her heart cheering,
     Unto my kingly castle."

PART THIRD.

" Arise, my daughter, it is time—
The king waits—'tis a merry rhyme—
   The banquet's ready; sure, I never
   Spake better for you—though I never
     Dared hope for such an honor."

" Array thyself, oh, sister mine:
In the king's courts their clothes are fine;
   Oh, very high you have sought your mate,
   And you leave me to my lonely fate—
     No matter—be but happy."

" Come, Dorothy, beloved one, come,
Your bridegroom waits, so only come.
   When you have entered the forest's shade
   You'll think no more of your home, my maid,
     Come, hasten, daughter, hasten."

" Mother, dear mother, tell me why
You take that knife? It makes me sigh."
   " The knife is sharp—in the forest deep
   I'll cut the eyes of a snake asleep.
     Come, hasten, daughter, hasten."

" Listen, dear sister, tell me why
You take that axe? It makes me sigh."
   " The axe is good—in the forest still,
   I'll maim a beast, a beast of ill-will.
     Come, hasten, sister, hasten."

And when they reached the forest dark
They said, "That snake, that beast, thou art!"
  The mountains and valleys wept to see
  How they killed the bride that was to be,
    That poor girl without blemish.

"Rejoice now in your stalwart groom;
Rejoice within your pleasant room;
  Look on him stately as a tower;
  Gaze on his brow in festive hour,
    You spinner, great in beauty."

"Dear mother, tell me what to do
With eyes and limbs, what shall I do?"
  "Don't leave them by the trunk, my daughter,
  Who knows but some one here might loiter—
    Yes, rather take them with you."

And when they left the forest shade
The mother said, "Be not afraid;
  You are alike—one like the other;
  Like two eyes from the selfsame mother.
    Take courage, then, my daughter."

And as they neared the castle gate,
The king was watching for his mate.
  He left the window, and went to meet,
  With his lords behind, his maiden sweet;
    He did not dream of treachery.

There was a wedding! Play on play,
The bride sat laughing all the day.
  There were banquets, music all the time;
  The world seemed to dance, to merry chime,
    Till the seventh day had passed.

And on the eighth day the king spake:
"Alas! my bride I must forsake.
  I must go and fight the haughty foe.
  Be happy, my bride, and let no woe
    Be thine till I come again.

" When from the battle I come back,
Our love will blossom without lack.
  Till then I bid thee diligent be:
  Spin thy flax, and keep thinking of me,
    As you spin the linen thread."

PART FOURTH

And in the forest dark and drear,
How sleeps the maid, I want to hear.
  From out six wounds her blood is gushing,
  And nought to still its awful rushing,
    As she lay on the emerald moss.

Gladly she went to meet her fate—
Now death is near her—it is late.
  Her body's cooling—her blood is set—
  Yes, even the ground with blood is wet,
    Alas, that you saw the king!

Behind a rock an old man came,
One could not tell from where he came;
  His long gray beard hung below his knees;
  He took up the murdered maid with ease,
    And carried her to his cell.

" Get up, my lad, the need is great—
  Take the gold spinning-wheel of fate;
  In the king's palace they will buy it;
  But hear: Only for feet I sell it,
    No other pay will answer."

The lad jumped on his fiery steed,
The spinning-wheel he held with heed.
" Who buys?" he called at the castle gate,
" Who would buy a spinning-wheel of fate,
    Of purest gold, I warrant?"

" Go, my mother, and ask the price,
  The spinning-wheel is strong and nice."
  " Buy it, my lady!   It is not dear—
  My father is cheap—you need not fear,
    For two feet he will give it."

" For two feet! 'Tis a strange, odd price—
Still I will buy—the wheel is nice.
 So mother bring our Dorothy's feet
 From out our room—let your steps be fleet—
  And I will take the spin-wheel."

The feet were given to the lad,
He rode back to the forest sad.
 " Hand me, my boy, the living water,
 I soon will heal this ill-starred daughter,
  Without a scar I'll heal her."

Wound upon wound he gently pressed;
It grew together like the rest,
 And the dead feet warmed with living heat,
 And grew to the body as was meet,
  And no scar was to be seen.

" Take, my boy, from the cupboard there,
The distaff—golden, very fair,
 In the king's palace they will buy it;
 But hear: Only for hands I sell it,
  No other pay will answer."

The lad jumped on his fiery steed,
The golden distaff he held with heed.
 The queen looked out of the window high,
 " If I had that distaff," she did sigh,
  " To match my golden spin-wheel."

" Get up, my mother, from your seat,
And ask the price of that distaff neat."
 " Buy it, my lady! It is not dear—
 My father is cheap—you need not fear,
  For two hands he will give it."

" For two hands! 'Tis a strange, odd price—
But I'll buy the distaff—it is nice.
 Go bring our Dorothy's hands, I pray,
 Though it seems to me 'tis hardly pay,
  For a golden distaff fine."

The hands were given to the lad,
He rode back to the forest sad.
  " Hand me, my boy, the living water,
  I soon will heal this ill-starred daughter,
    Without a scar, I'll heal her."

Wound upon wound he gently pressed;
It grew together like the rest,
  And the dead hands warmed with living heat,
  And grew to the body as was meet,
    But no scar was to be seen.

" Up, my lad, and be on the way,
I have a whirl to sell this day;
  In the king's palace they will buy it;
  But listen: Only for eyes I sell it,
    No other pay will answer."

The lad jumped on his fiery steed,
The precious whirl he held with heed.
  The queen looked out of the window high,
  " If I had that whirl "—and she did sigh,
    " To match my golden distaff.

" Get up, my mother, from your seat,
And ask the price of that whirl so neat! "
  " For eyes, my lady!   The whirl to-day,
  'Tis my father's will, I must obey,
    For two eyes you can have it."

" For two eyes!   Are you crazy, lad?
Who is your father, speak out, lad? "
  " Who is my father, you need not know,
  Those who seek him, find him not I know,
    But he'll come to you I ween."

" Mother, mother, what shall I say?
I must have that whirl—come what may! "
  " So bring our Dorothy's eyes, I pray;
  I must have that whirl this very day,
    Give him our Dorothy's eyes."

The eyes were given to the lad,
He rode back to the forest sad.
" Hand me, my boy, the living water,
  I soon will heal this ill-starred daughter,
    Without a scar I'll heal her."

He placed the eyes where they should be;
Life came back, and the girl could see,
  And the maiden rose, and looked around—
  She was alone—not even a sound
    Disturbed the forest's silence.

PART FIFTH.

Three weeks had passed, the king rode home,
Merrily back upon his roan.
" How are you, beloved wife," he said,
" And have you been spinning linen thread,
    And thinking of me, my love?"

" Your parting words I kept with care—
  Look at this golden spin-wheel fair,
    The only spin-wheel of gold, I trow,
    With distaff and whirl I bought it now,
      For love of you I bought it."

" I pray thee sit and spin, my dove,
  A golden thread spin me, my love."
    With joy she sat herself down to spin,
    Turned the wheel—then blanched, her face grew
      thin,
      As she heard that awful song.

" Vrrr—you have spun an awful thread—
  Yes, blood is on your hands and head—
    You killed your sister, and took her place.
    You tore her limbs and eyes from their place.
      Vrrr—you have spun an awful thread."

" What spinning wheel is this, I pray?
  Strange is the song it sings, I say?
    But spin on, my wife, I fain would hear
    Some more of this song, so strange and drear,
      Spin—my wife, spin on, I pray."

" Vrrr—you have spun an awful thread!
  Through treachery you are now wed;
      You killed your sister, and took her place!
      Yes, you tore her eyes from out her face!
          Vrrr—you have spun an awful thread! "

" Ho! dreadful is this song to me!
  You are not wife what you should be,
      But spin, I bid thee, for the third time;
      Let me hear once more that dreadful rhyme;
          Spin, my wife—spin on, I say."

" Vrrr—you have spun an awful thread!
  Through treachery you are now wed;
      In the wood your murdered sister lies—
      You cheated the king with shameful lies.
          Vrrr—you have spun an awful thread! "

The king heard, and he rushed away,
On steed he sprang and went his way.
    In the forest vast he wandered far,
    And he called her name near and afar,
    "Dorothy, where art thou, love?"

PART SIXTH.

Forest, castle, a stretching plain—
Two riders ride along amain.
    The bridegroom and bride ride on with speed,
    One hears the horseshoes ring at their speed,
        As they ride to the castle.

And a wedding was held once more—
The bride was fairer than before.
    There were banquets, music all the time,
    The world seemed to dance to merry chime,
        Till three weeks had pass'd away.

And what of that raven mother?
And cruel, cruel sister?
    Four foxes run in the forest dark,
    Each one has a woman's trunk for part,
        As they rush into the wood.

The heads hang down withont the eyes,
The hands and feet are cut likewise.
   'n the forest dark, they met their fate,
   Where they killed the maid they met their fate,
     The death they made her suffer.

And what of the gold spinning wheel?
Its song was done—that golden wheel
   Sang but three times that miserable lay,
   Then, strange to say, it vanished away.
     But where no man can tell you.

CHRISTMAS.

In the holy Christmas season
  Shines the moonlight bright and clear,
In the graveyard, on the crosses,
  In the warden's window near;
And the moonlight roused his slumber—
  From his bed he rose in haste,
Thinking it must be now morning
  And he had no time to waste.

Bright the snow is lying round him,
  As he goes to ring the bell.
When he hears the church clock striking
  Twelve o'clock, he counts it well.
Home again he would have turned him,
  Lain him down in peace again,
When by chance he sees the window,
  Where light streams from out the pane.

Lost in wonder he went onward
  To the church, and entered in.
Candles by the altar burning
  Light the church's outline dim.
There he sees upon the benches,
  Men and women scattered round,
People that he knows are kneeling,
  Praying there without a sound.

Then he spoke, and said " Good-morning,"
  First to this one, then to that.
Not an answer did they give him,
  No one noticed where he sat

Then a chill of horror shook him—
  And his hair it stood on ends.
With his thoughts in wild confusion
  From the church his steps he bends.

To the priest he goes, and wildly
  Tells him of the wondrous tale.
Though astonished the priest calmly
  Speaks of God who cannot fail.
" See this wild fear we must conquer."
  Holy water now he takes,
Sprinkles it upon them saying,
" God will save us for His sake."

To the church he bends his footsteps,
  With his own eyes now to see,
While the warden half-dead follows,
  That strange sight once more to see.
And there truly, he can see them,
  People that he knows full well,
At the altar they are gazing,
  They are praying, one can tell.

Not one turns to look about him,
  They are praying with a will.
As the clock strikes one, the shadows
  Pass away in silence chill.
Here it changes, there it changes,
  And the lights fade one by one;
Then the scene grows dim and faded,
  Like a dream that now is done.

Little time had passed, and several
  Went from out this world away;
Then another one was bidden
  All his farewells quick to say;
And before the year was finished
  Every one that they had seen
Had been called by God Almighty,
  To a brighter, happier scene.

Then they both knew what the meaning
  Of this strange scene did imply,
And upon each Christmas midnight
  To the church they went to spy,
Who of all their living neighbors
  To the grave was drawing near,
For not one that they saw praying
  Would outlive the coming year.

And one year they looked with horror—
  Thought it was the Judgment day!
For the church was filled with people
  Sitting, crowding all the way;
And they could not count the number—
  Filled were they with horror great.
But next year the plague came raging,
  Many people met their fate.

And as once they went to notice
  Who should die the coming year,
With a start of inward terror
  Saw the warden, himself near.
He was kneeling by the threshold—
  And the priest the mass did say—
Then they knew, beyond all doubting,
  This year they should pass away.

Then they knelt in earnest prayer,
  While the priest, his hands upraised,
Saying, " Oh, Almighty Father,
  Be Thy name forever praised!
Grant that death may find us worthy
  Of that heaven Thou hast won."
And the warden answered humbly,
" Father, let Thy will be done."

And they praised the Lord while living,
  Lying down, and getting up;
Giving to the poor and needy,
  What they had on plate and cup.
Very heedful of their footsteps,
  Not to miss the narrow way,
And before the year was finished
  Both in God had passed away.

THE ORPHAN.

" Whose child is this that in the wintry storm,
  The cutting north-wind, with its snow and ice,
At midnight in the graveyard walks forlorn,
  And seeks a grave amidst the snow and ice?"

" Mother, oh my loving mother, hear me,
  Your little daughter calls, oh hear me now;
I am forsaken of all men, I see;
  Since father died, how wretched I am now.

" Nothing but hunger and neglect are mine;
  Look where I will, no friendly face I see;
Oh, look in pity on me, mother mine,
  Oh loving mother, let me come to thee."

The little child wept, and the pearly tears
  Froze on her cheeks like diamonds clear and bright;
Upon her mother's grave she slept, no fears
  Came to disturb her, 'twas a sad, sad sight.

The snow fell fast upon the childlike form,
  But see, she dreamt a very happy dream;
She heard her mother's voice, and saw her form
  Stoop down to take her—Could it be a dream?

The child slept on, no need now to awake—
  In that glad dream the soul had passed away;
Where she had slept they now her grave must make;
  Ah! woe is me, it was a sad, sad day.

BŘETISLAV.

Before the gate a harper stands,
　And begs that he may enter in.
" 'Tis well to praise one's native land,
　And hear its songs.　Yes, let him in,
Open the gate and let him sing,
That every idle care take wing."
　Thus ordered the prince Oldřich.

The singer entered, young of mein,
　And lowly bowed before the prince.
Then stooping low, he kissed the seam
　Of Božena's dress, wife of the prince.
Before the golden throne he stood,
And struck the harp with tones that would
　But make his song the sweeter.

" A rich young man once loved a girl,
　A maid without compare;
But cloister walls they hid his pearl,
　His heart was in despair.

" How many weary days he spent
　In wandering round the walls;
Then in a happy hour he went,
　And sang before those halls.

" ' Oh, rosy lips, what say ye now,
　Within that cloister cold?
Look from thy window, see me now,
　A minstrel singing bold.'

" ' Oh listen,' said a far-off voice,
   ' Singer, of lovely song;
  Take out your sword and be your choice,
   To save me from this throng.'

" ' Oh, thanks be to that simple song!
   Oh, thanks be to the sky!
  My life I'll give to right thy wrong,
   Or very gladly die.'

" He went and donned a pilger robe,
   Then came with footsteps slow;
  One could not see beneath that robe
   The sabre hanging low.

" He found them singing a sweet hymn,
   While on their knees they prayed.
  He stood awhile and heard their hymn—
   Hand on his sword he laid.

" On to the church they singing went,
   Chanting ' Zion! Zion!'
  With one bound in their midst he went,
   Like a roaring lion.

" Between the shrieks and screams of fear,
   He caught the girl he loved.
  Then turned him to the drawbridge near,
   Carrying the maid he loved.

" The keeper of the drawbridge saw,
   And would have stopped their flight.
  He drew the bridge up, 'twas his law,
   To have the chain draw right.

" The youth drew out his mighty sword,
   He cut the chain in two.
  The links were severed by his sword,
   And on the bridge they flew.

" The keeper of the bridge stood pale,
   The nuns were sore afraid;
The servants they set up a wail,
   But all that did not aid.

" I wonder if you now can tell,
   Who was this youth so bold?
Who cut the strong chain quick and well,
   With lady in his hold?"

The harper ceased, his song was done,
   And low he bowed before the throne.
The youths they whispered every one,
   " It is not true," in undertone;
" For who can cut an iron chain,
   E'en with a sword that hath no stain?
   The singer singeth nonsense."

Prince Oldřich smiled, and asked his wife,
   Božena, if she knew his thought?
" It seems to me 'tis true to life,
   And that the youth his loved one sought.
I feel that Břetislav, our son,
Could do this deed beneath the sun,
   As well as that bold stripling."

And see the door flew open wide,
   While youth and maiden entered in.
They bow, and to his father's side
   Břetislav leads his loved one in.
" Yes father, you are right, your son
Did do this deed, beneath the sun,
   To win his loved one, Jitka."

A BOHEMIAN LEGEND.

The little child stood on the bench,
  And cried as loud as child can cry.
" Will you be quiet, naughty one—
  That is the way that gypsies cry.

" Twelve o'clock will soon be striking,
  And see the dinner is not done;
What will father say, you spoilt one,
  When my work lies there all undone.

" Hush! here are your playthings—wagon,
  Horses, soldiers, whatever you will."
Scarcely had she finished speaking,
  All was thrown away with a will.

And the child began its howling,
  Shrieking out like a thing possessed;
" Hush! hush!" cried the tired mother,
  " So cry souls that die unconfessed.

" Come witch—come and take her naughty—
  Hush! hush! or I will call the witch.
Come witch, come and take her naughty—
  Oh, good God! can that be the witch?"

Little humpback, horrible form,
  Half revealed by the ample cloak,
In the room on crutches hobbling,
  Came the witch; her voice was a croak.

" Give me the child." " Oh Holy Christ,
  Forgive my sins," the mother cried.
" Ah, never from the room the witch
  Will go, till one of us has died."

She nears the table where they stand,
　She creeps along as shadows creep.
The wretched mother hardly breathes—
　She clasps her child, that does not weep.

Alas! alas! that fatal call;
　Poor child, there is no help for thee.
The witch comes creeping, creeping on,
　She stretches out her hand for thee.

She stretches out her hand to take—
　The mother cannot keep her hold.
" I pray ye by Christ's wounds," she calls,
　But still she cannot keep her hold.

And senseless to the ground she falls,
　Just as the clock begins to strike.
The father from his work comes home,
　The look of things he does not like.

They brought the mother to herself—
　But oh, the child upon her breast,
The little child she loved so well,
　Had passed away to endless rest.

THE GENTLEMAN FROM LKOUŠE, 1571.

Šamonice's bells are gladly ringing—
The farmers mourn, but their lords are laughing.

From out the castle to the church they go,
Lorecký Lkouše has two sons, you know.

Carriage on carriage drive from out the gate.
The gentleman of Lkouše looks elate.

He oft had thought to die without an heir,
Now he drives through the village with a pair.

But see, the way is blocked with village men,
And Peter Dulík stops the steeds just then.

Širák bows, and fain would now have spoken.
Šamonický waits not, calls out " Open! "

" Coachman, beat the knave! Whip him from the way!
Let my horses tramp them down this glad day."

But Peter Dulík will not loose his hold,
But calls out in a voice both loud and bold:

" God has given you twins—will you mercy show,
Mercy, for God's sake, mercy to us show.

" Free us from the tenth part—lighten our way,
For we starve and fast, as on Good Friday.

" Faint we are with labor—toiling for you—
Oh, bless us this day—twins God gave to you!"

" Yes, God gave me twins !" Lorecký now cried,
" They will be whips for your lazy hide.

" They will help me drive you rascals, low born—
To help me in this task, see, they were born.

" Two God gave to me, one was not enough—
To dare to speak of mercy, and such stuff.

" Wait till they grow up—Clear the way I say,
And take care that we meet no more to-day."

Dulík dropped the reins and all turned aside;
Dazed he looked around, wrath he could not hide.

Then he quickly spoke in the common speech,
" Never as whips will your son's manhood reach.

" No more we will murmur—this we will do,
Cut your whips before they grow strong and true.

" For our children's backs scorpions we'll not rear—
Nor see them made to cripples—have no fear! "

Šamonice's   bells are gladly ringing—
The lords mourn, but the farmers are laughing.

The castle is in flames—blood is flowing,
On a cask Peter Dulík is judging.

With pitchforks round about him stood the men,
It was the farmer's sigh of justice then.

Beneath him in a pool of blood there lay
Šamonice's   lord, with his sons that day.

THE YOUTH FROM HRUŠOV.

" Across the stony mountains,
    Who comes in war's array?
The warlike Zvikoš is it?
    Quick, arm thee for the fray.
A charger waits to bear thee—
    My son, grasp quick thy sword,
And hold the spear with courage,
    I am too old for that horde."

Thus spake the old Hrušovec
    Unto his well-loved son,
And gave unto his brave hand,
    A flagstaff bravely won.
" Take now this golden banner,
    'Neath which your grandsire fought
The heathen on the seacoast,
    Where he great havoc wrought.

" Many a time this castle
    The enemy had won,
But when they saw this banner,
    They feared it, every one.
Take it, my son, and cherish,
    Yea, as thou wouldst thy life—
Come back with it triumphing,
    Or die there in the strife."

The old man's voice was husky,
    The lad from him must part—
The youth he caught the banner,
    And pressed it to his heart;

Upon his breast was harness,
  His sword was by his side;
His heart beat for his loved one,
  With love he could not hide.

Her eyes with tears are heavy,
  As she looks on the youth;
Her cheeks are pale with anguish,
" God be with thee in sooth."
A wreath upon the banner,
  A ribbon on the sword,
Then she called out, " Be prosperous,
  Come, living from the horde."

One heard the noise of battle,
  The blows that fell apace;
New warriors rush to conquer,
  To fill the vacant place;
The youth is with them, carrying
  The banner of his land,
The sun is shining on them,
  It lights the bloody band.

Upon the castle turret,
  The maiden gazing stands;
She looks down on her lover,
  Fighting those warlike bands;
Her heart with pleasure beating,
  When high the banner flies;
Her hands to heaven she raises,
  When low the banner lies.

Like a wild beast defending
  The lair that is his home,
The youth is rushing onward,
  His horse is all in foam.
But Zvikoš goes to meet him,
  He strikes with might and main,
The arm that holds the banner,
  The hand sinks down in pain.

THE YOUTH FROM HRUŠOV.

The banner would have sunk now,
  Had not the fearless youth
Caught it in his strong left hand,
  And held it high in truth.
A lion was the stripling
  In bravery; to and fro
One saw the banner waving
  Like forest tree, I trow.

Zvikoš' men are charging—
  One comes behind the lad,
With mighty spear he strikes him;
  His blood is running sad;
The left hand now is shattered,
  The flag with blood is red—
His pale lips caught the banner—
  The horse turned round and fled.

Fled onward to the castle,
  And there the youth fell dead;
His pale lips held the banner—
  The noble soul had fled.
The maiden on the turret,
  Like stricken doe, runs down,
She looks upon her lover,
  Then dead she too falls down.

The plain is green with grasses,
  A mighty tree stands bare;
The lightning struck it often,
  For ages it stood there.
The castle is a ruin—
  It frowns down from the hill,
But the memory of the youth
  Lives in Bohemia still.

THE DAUGHTER'S CURSE.

" Why are you so lost in thinking,
        Daughter mine?
Why are you so lost in thinking?
You who were so fond of laughing—
    And whose face was always glad!"

" I have killed a little pigeon,
        Mother mine;
I have killed a little pigeon,
A forsaken little pigeon;
    It was white; ah, white like snow."

" 'Twas no pigeon, I misdoubt me,
        Daughter mine;
'Twas no pigeon, I misdoubt me;
But your brain is touched, I fear me,
    And your look is strange and wild."

" Oh, I have killed a little child,
        Mother mine;
Oh, I have killed a little child;
My new-born babe, my own fair child—
    Would I could die with remorse!"

" What do you mean to do, I ask,
        Daughter mine?
What do you mean to do, I ask?
How will you mend this luckless task—
    How will you find God's mercy?"

" I will go seek that flower now,
        Mother mine;
I will go seek that flower now;
That soon will cool my criminal brow,
    And stop my pulses throbbing."

" And when you find the grass you seek,
        Daughter mine;
And when you find the grass you seek;
The flax that grows beside the leek
    In many a garden round? "

" Behind the bridge, upon the hill,
        Mother mine;
Behind the bridge, upon the hill,
In tree I'll drive a nail with will,
    And so end all my sinning."

" What last word will you leave the youth,
        Daughter mine?
What last word will you leave the youth
Who used to come to us, forsooth,
    And loved thee for a season? "

" A blessing on his head, I pray,
        Mother mine;
A blessing on his head, I pray—
Remorse until his dying day,
    Because he lightly wooed me."

" What last word do you leave to me,
        Daughter mine?
What last word do you leave to me,
Who loved you when a baby wee—
    And who brought thee up with toil?"

" My curse I leave thee, that is all,
        Mother mine;
My curse I leave thee, that is all,
That you may know no peace at all,
    Because you let me have my way."

THE STORY OF A NEW MOTHER.

His mother died when he was but a child;
His saintly mother, with her features mild,
Was laid away in the cold churchyard soil,
Ere yet his little hands had learned to toil,
And soon his father took another wife,
A buxom maiden, who was fond of strife,
And bore illwill to the poor little lad,
Whose childish life she made most drear and sad.
One day his childish heart was full to break,
And childishly he asked, " When will she wake?
Oh, tell me, father, will she ever wake—
My own loved mother?   Wake up, for my sake?"
" Alas! my son, she sleepeth in the grave,
Beside the churchyard gate, where grasses wave.
Oh, they sleep well who sleep within the soil—
Go play in peace, my son, she knows no toil."
With toddling feet he to the churchyard went,
And sitting on her grave, his strength outspent,
Began to think how he should wake her sleep,
Who slept in the cold earth so well and deep.
With a large pin he loosed the graveyard soil,
And was so eager in his loving toil
He was not startled when he heard her voice,
Calling to him, " My child, my love, my choice,
I cannot come to thee, for on my heart
Lies a great stone, from which I cannot part.
But tell me, my beloved, why art thou here?"
And then the little child, without a fear,
Said to his mother, " When she gives me bread,
She always says she wishes I were dead.
You also gave me bread, oh, mother mine,
And buttered it, for surely I was thine.

When she combs my hair, see my tears fall fast,
For she pulls it till the blood comes at last;
When you combed my curls, oft you kissed my hair,
And you loved to hear me called good and fair;
When she washes me with her rough, hard hand,
See, she sometimes scrubs me, yea, e'en with sand;
When you washed me, oh, never did I cry.
Oh, how can you sleep, and leave me to cry?"
Then his mother's voice said low, "So, my son,
I will come for thee at the rising sun."
Then the little child, with a happy smile,
Said to his father, " In a little while
You can dig my grave by my mother's side;
By this time to-morrow I shall have died;
For she told me true, at the rising sun
I will come and take thee, my darling son."
When the morning came, dead upon his bed
Lay the little child, but his soul had fled
To those realms on high, where his mother stood—
No need of speaking, all was understood.
On the third sad day, by his mother's side
They laid him gently, who so oft had sighed,
And his father, gazing upward at the sky,
Said, "Oh, would to God, that I too could die."

THE MYSTERIOUS RINGING.

The winter evening draweth near—
O'er stubble fields the wind howls drear,
And borne upon the northern blast
To Karluv Týn rides a courier fast.

The tower bell rings sad to-day,
Without is frost, within is May;
The servants they are happy all,
And oft a merry jest let fall.

The tower ringer enters now,
An old man with a noble brow;
Still round him gather all the youth,
Like children for some news forsooth.

The old man sinks within his seat;
Sad is his look, though mild and sweet;
The youth stand round him waiting still,
To hear his tale, or do his will.

Oh, sad the news I have to tell—
* Our loved king Charles, he is not well—
Pray, children, that he may recover;
Charles whom we love, yea, like no other.

Long he has suffered fever's pain—
Oh, would that he were well again!
Oh, God in mercy, save our king,
Save our good Charles, oh, spare our king.

---

* NOTE.—Charles the Fourth, king of Bohemia, A.D. 1347
to 1378, Emperor of the Romans.

A Christian! At St. Catherine's shrine,
Each year he prayed the King divine
To bless his people; this good king
Without God never did a thing.

He loved Bohemia from his heart—
As king, as father took her part.
He loved us all like children dear,
Our good, good Charles, without a peer.

What's that? You hear? The key hangs there—
The tower's shut—Let the light flare.
You hear? How mournful is the tone—
St. Catherine's bell—it rings alone!"

Silence awhile, they listen all,
The bell tolls from the tower tall,
Then suddenly the bells ring all.
And strange the message that they bore.
" He is no more—he is no more."

A wonder—why the key hangs there—
" Bring me a light, I'll climb the stair."
Breathless he stands before the door,
The bells are ringing as before.

The door is shut! he listening stands—
The bells are rung by unknown hands;
He trembles as he listening stands,
For sad the message that they bore:
" He is no more—he is no more."

The ringer opens quick the door,
He climbs up to the turret floor;
But there he breathless stands in fear,
The bells toll, but no man is near.

He hears their iron hearts beat quick—
The melody it makes him sick;
He gazes round in mute despair,
For not a living soul is there.

He falls upon his knees and prays,
The great bell far above him sways,
Then all ring, like on funeral days.
He listens, praying on the floor,
" Charles is no more!   Charles is no more!"

The next day came a rider, sent
From Prague to Karlův Týn sadly spent;
And as he spoke the people wept—
Yes, sadly wept—for Charles now slept.

They wept to hear their king was dead;
He died the night before, they said.
Bohemia honors still his name,
Their good King Charles, well known to fame.

INVITATION TO SONG.

Oh, let us sing songs full of love,
   Bohemian national songs of love;
For as long as Bohemians sing,
   Their national life cannot take wing.
Go wander all over our land,
   Over valley and wood-crowned hill,
There's not a place without a band,
   Or song, like a mountain rill.

The Bohemian lion loved song—
   Songs he sang against every wrong;
And when for his country he fought,
   It was also with song that he taught.
Even the castle Vyšehrad
   Shook when Záboj the minstrel sang,
Like Orfej, upon the green sod,
   War songs that like clear trumpets rang.
For this reason Bohemians should sing,
   That their national life n'er take wing.

SWEET DEATH.

A youth rides quickly on his steed—
    He rides to battle.
The war-horse gladly neighs and leaps,
But his poor mother at home weeps,
    For her darling son,
    For her darling son.

" Weep not, weep not, my loved mother,
    For your dearest son;
I must go, you all to defend,
And my loved country's flag attend,
    Even if I die,
    Even if I die.

" After a time I'll come again,
    On my battle steed.
Bohemians cannot cowards be,
But the thick of the battle see,
    Both I and my steed,
    Both I and my steed.

" But should I in battle sinking
    N'er come home again,
Then remember, mother dearest,
No Bohemian ever fearest
    For his land to die,
    For his land to die."

SONG OF A SOLDIER.

Very soon ended the dream of my life—
    Yesterday I galloped gladly,
    To-day my heart's blood ⁓ushes madly,
To-morrow I sleep in death,
To-morrow I sleep in death.
    Tra, la, la, la.

Your boyhood and youth have ended too soon;
    You had a soldier's brow of pride,
    And your cheeks were like the roses dyed;
They have faded now, alas!
They have faded now, alas!
    Tra, la, la, la.

Know no fear—let the will of God be done;
    Write about me a warrior's song,
    That I was brave and did no wrong;
I die gladly for my land,
I die gladly for my land,
    Tra, la, la, la.

WHY IS IT.

The peaceful moon is shining,
  In heaven's vaulted dome;
The stars around her shining,
  Like sisters of one home.
Why, oh why, poor heart of mine,
Art thou troubled and dost pine?

Upon the glassy lake's surface
  A swan majestic swims;
Rushes in this quiet place
  Obey the zephyr's whims.
Why, oh why, poor heart of mine,
Art thou troubled and dost pine?

A pretty pigeon flutters,
  Soft cooing, to his dove;
Mother swallow chirping flutters,
  Seeking food for her love.
Why, oh why, poor heart of mine,
Art thou troubled and dost pine?

Day and night I pass in anguish,
  In an endless warfare;
Nothing pleases me; I languish,
  And my heart is in despair.
Why, oh why, poor heart of mine,
Art thou troubled and dost pine?

The melancholy nightingale
  Is singing of his pain;
I too have lost my love and wail—
  My tears they fall like rain.
This is the reason, heart of mine,
That thou art troubled and dost pine.

.

WHEN I WENT TO SEE YOU.

When I went to see you through the forest—
  Ah, alas! through the forest—
You were more lively then, more lively then,
  Ah, alas! more lively then.
But now you are pale, my loved one;
But now you are pale, my loved one;
And I fear for your ail there is no cure;
  Ah, alas! there is no cure.

When I went to see you by the marshes—
  Ah, alas! by the marshes—
You were like a rose then, like a rose then,
  Ah, alas! like a rose then.
But now you are pale, my loved one;
But now you are pale, my loved one;
And I fear for your ail there is no cure;
  Ah, alas! there is no cure.

When I went to see you, 'neath the window—
  Ah, alas! neath the window—
You were all milk and rose, all milk and rose,
  Ah, alas! all milk and rose.
But now you are pale, my loved one;
But now you are pale, my loved one;
And I fear for your ail there is no cure;
  Ah, alas! there is no cure.

AT THE CHURCH DOOR.

He—Now they lead my loved one to the church door;
    Now then you are mine, beloved,
    Now you are mine.

She—Not yet am I yours, loved, not yet;
    I am still my mother's own.

He—Now they lead my loved one to the altar;
    Now then you are mine, beloved,
    Now you are mine.

She—Not yet am I yours, beloved, not yet;
    I am still my mother's own.

He—Now I lead my loved one from the altar;
    Now then you are mine, beloved,
    Now you are mine.

She—Now then I am yours, beloved, alone;
    Now I am no more mamma's.

CUCKOO SONG.

" Cuckoo, cuckoo," sang the cuckoo
  In the little grove,
  Ah, in the little grove.
In her own home wept my loved one
  In her lonely room,
  Ah, in her lonely room.

" Why are you weeping, lamenting—
  Surely you are mine,
  Ah, surely you are mine.
When the cuckoo cries at Christmas
  Three times you are mine,
  Ah, three times you are mine."

" How can I keep from lamenting—
  When you are not mine,
  Ah, when you are not mine.
For the cuckoo ne'er at Christmas
  Lets his voice be heard,
  Ah, lets his voice be heard."

GOOD-NIGHT.

Good-night, my beloved,
　　Sweet, good-night.
God watch you Himself, loved,
　　And keep you.
　　Dear, good-night,
　　And sleep well.
May your dreams be sweet, my beloved.

Good-night my beloved,
　　Sweet, good-night,
God watch you Himself, loved,
　　And keep you,
　　Dear, good-night,
　　And sleep well.
May ¬our dreams be of me, my beloved.

ARE NOT, ARE NOT.

Are not, are not,
　What you would seem to be,
Are not, are not,
　True as you seem to be.
Your heart is false, I see,
And you care nought for me.
But once, but once, you will regret.

Care not, care not,
　If you love me or no.
Care not, care not,
　If you forsake.
Such a lover as you
I can find not a few,
Better, better than such as you.

IT IS GOD'S WILL.

It is according to God's will
That what we love the most must fade,
        Or forsake.
There's nothing that our hearts so fill
With sorrow as when loved things fade,
        Or forsake,
        Or forsake.

If a young lassie, full of grace,
Should chance to give you a rosebud,
        Remember,
To-morrow will smile in your face,
But at eve is dead, the rosebud,
        Remember,
        Remember.

If God has then blessed you with love,
And you worship a lassie true,
        From your heart,
There'll come still a time when your love
Will forsake you, and not be true,
        But forsake,
        But forsake.

BEAUTIFUL STARS.

Oh, beautiful bright stars,
    How very small you are.
Once you used to give me pleasure,
Once you used to give me pleasure,
    The whole live-long evening.

One of you the brightest,
    The glorious morning star,
Followed me with its golden light,
Followed me with its golden light,
    To the home of my love.

Moon amidst the high clouds,
    How far off you are!
So far off is my beloved one,
So far off is my beloved one,
    From my reach as you are.

GOING A-WOOING.

When our Vit went a-wooing,
Down the winding lane,
Not a cloud was in the sky
To betoken rain.
In his best clothes he went wooing,
Starched-up shirt and collar showing
Now a decent lad goes wooing
While a bachelor still.

When he came back from his wooing
'Twas a-pouring rain;
Drenched he was from head to foot—
That did give him pain.
Soaking wet was all his clothing,
And they mocked him well for going,
While they looked at him with loathing
In his sorry plight.

Poor young man, this had not happened
Had he stayed at home,
After a coquettish maid
It is hard to roam.
While she frowned upon his wooing,
See this happened to him, showing
One must be quite sure of winning,
Or the girl may mock.

MADE OF THE EARTH.

Made of the earth, to earth I came
    And on the earth my senses found,
Well contented that the same
    Earth should be my burying ground.
        Lord make me happy then,
        Lord make me happy then.

Where, ah, where, are the loving hands
    Of my long-lost tender mother,
Who rocked me with hopeful hands
    And loved me as no other.
        When I was a wee one,
        When I was a wee one.

They are no more, alas! no more!
    Long they sleep in the cold, dark earth;
How forget the love they bore
    To me, and their honest worth.
        How thank all their goodness,
        How thank all their goodness.

THE RAIN.

It rained so hard, a dreadful rain,
   And it was muddy,
   Ah, so very muddy.
Still I used to go and see you
   In spite of all that,
   Ah, in spite of all that.
The more I loved you true, and well,
The falser were you, sad to tell;
   That was all the thanks,
   Ah, that was all the thanks.

The nightingale is a small bird
   Very hard to catch,
   Ah, very hard to catch.
A lover's eyes are quick to see
   And won't be deceived,
   Ah, and won't be deceived.
Before you will play false to me,
I'll choose a soldier's life and be
   A warrior free,
   Ah, maid, so false to me.

Do you dream me sorrow-stricken?
   Weighed by heartaches down,
   Ah, weighed by heartaches down.
Have I asked you for your daughter?
   That you think me blind,
   Ah, that you think me blind.
There are maidens all too many,
Like the berries on the holly,
   When one looks around,
   Ah, when one looks around.

PRAYER ON THE MOUNTAIN ŘIP.

Tired, fatigued, and half unconscious,
    Pilgrims from a famished country,
From a land of sighs and wailing,
    We pray, sire Čech, for our country.

Bless, that our father's strength may increase,
    That our infant children may grow strong.
Bless, that our skulls be hard as thy rocks,
    To withstand the evil and wrong,

From a persecuted land we call,
    Where the terrible fiend we must gorge—
Where the Dragon is master of all,
    We beseech thee, help us, St. George!

Give us strength that we may do our work,
    That each be filled from on high with strength.
That like yon we may kill the Dragon
    With a spear, and conquer at length.

From the mountain top where we can see
    For miles, let the victorious hymn sound,
For our country again it is free,
    And ours every valley and mound.

p. 30

COMFORT.

Mortal, if this earthly sorrow,
　Loss and anguish crush thy heart,
If thy friends forsake and hate thee;
　If thy children break thy heart,
If no wish of thine should prosper—
　Find fulfillment in this life;
And the good you planned and strove for
　Die unknown in the strife,
Still I bid thee hope and suffer,
　Hope in God, and leave thy care—
He will lay no more upon thee
　Than He gives thee strength to bear.
So, poor heart, new courage taking,
　Let what will, with thee betide,
Knowing that thy God is mighty,
　And Thy Father by thy side.

SONGS OF THE HEAVENS.

SONG I.

Oh, most beautiful summer night,
Enraptured my soul with thy light;
    In the daytime 'tis suffocating,
    But evening is invigorating.

From the vaulted heavens, the moon,
Heaven's old father, very soon,
    With silvery light all over the world,
    Will shine, changing water to pearl.

Around him then his children small,
The little stars good-hearted all,
    With their golden voices seem to say,
    To-morrow will be a lovely day.

SONG VI.

Believe me, the bright stars also feel pain,
Much, very much, troubles them sore—
And they feel, and can condole with our pain,
    In this tearful vale of sorrow.

They also have their work, around the sun,
Round, round they spin, and glide and shine;
About a hundred thousand miles they run,
    Paid only by a span of life.

They also have to work themselves to death,
And martyrize their golden forms.
The bright haze we sometimes see is their breath,
    Which we vaguely call falling stars.

SONG XII.

All the bright, fiery stars,
    That cluster round the moon.
Once flew away from the sun
    To shine on our world like stars,
But they were cradled in the sun.

All the bright, fiery stars,
    After their destined time,
Must fly away from our sky,
    For the sun will be their grave,
And there the gleaming stars shall die.

SONG XXXVII.

The voice of the prophet said,
    That all that live must also die.
Oh, yes, we know 'tis truth he said—
    Before the world dies, we must die.

Whatever blooms will also fade—
    What comes to earth, must from earth go—
The world's poor knowledge, it will fade,
    Like any white rose that doth blow.

And so the thought of death should not
    Stab our poor weary human heart.
We live, and outlive, 'tis our lot
    Examples to be, 'tis our part.

Before birth, we knew not the earth—
    Nor know we now its secret power.
We cannot even know our earth—
    What know we of God's mighty power.

And should calamity overtake
  Our world—well, God is mighty still.
He still can save us for His sake,
  All might is His, if He but will.

We know that we must die—so live
  That when we die our lowly grave
Be honored by the souls that live,
  Let fame attend us to our grave.

HAPPINESS AND MISERY.

Oh, happiness, happiness,
  Is a fair flower.
Ah, the more 'tis a pity
  Its roots last an hour.

Comes a wind, it is broken,
  Water has power
To spoil it without pity,
  It lasts but an hour.

Oh, misery, misery,
  Most bitter thy root.
From thee never a flower
  Nor leaf, nor green shoot.

Oh, how many, how many
  The heart that must ache,
At hopes unattainable,
  And at last must break.

.

SELF SOUGHT.

The sweetest kernel is always
   The one we have broken ourselves;
The gold that we prize the highest
   Is the one we have delved ourselves.

The pearl that we count the purest
   We have robbed ourselves from the sea,
And the truth we count the dearest
   Must be inborn and make us free.

.

TRUTH MUST CONQUER.

There were always people ready
   To prevent the sun from rising;
Still the sun did rise in splendor,
   Rise in spite of all their railing.

Yes, he rose in glory shining
   On the high hills, the plains, the vales,
Rose in splendor on the countries,
   On the blue ocean full of sails.

I REMIND YOU.

Say, will there come a time when the rich man
Will be ashamed of his good clothes and say,
I see my brother man, without a roof,
Shivering and cold upon this wintry day.
Say, will there come a time when he will pause,
And throw away his goblet ere he drink,
And think unto himself, my fellow men,
For want of bread, around me in death sink.

And when the Holy night, the birth of Christ
Brings to the wealthy child the Christmas tree,
Ladened with gifts, and lights, the poor man's child,
In his poor room, says sadly, " Naught for me?"
Naught but the flowers on his frost-bound pane.
Is this the love of neighbor, like one's self?
Oh, Christ of God, Thy Kingdom is not yet,
We are not ruled by love, but filthy pelf.

Oh, that Thy kingdom, nearer to our earth,
Thy starry kingdom, would draw near in love,
And teach our human hearts to know and feel
The blessedness of helping man above,
The degradation that makes life a hell.
Oh, write upon your banners, " Help the poor."
Light the sad eyes, and chase away the care;
He will reward you, who was also poor.

THE BOHEMIAN MOTHER'S TALE.

He was not like the other boys,
  Who only cared for noisy plays;
He used to throw away his toys,
  And lie there dreaming half his days.
     He was an idle lad,
     Who would not learn at school;
But I can't say that he was bad,
     Beyond the rule.

He was not strong enough to work,
  To do the drudgery of the farm;
His father's words they seemed to hurt,
  Though, heaven knows, he meant no harm.
     The boy would flush with pain,
     At every angry tone;
I've often watched him through the lane
     Walk off alone.

A boy like that can never live,
  And thrive, in such a home as ours;
I therefore thought 'tis best to give
  A boy like that to higher powers.
     Within the convent gate
     I led my wayward son,
Right thankful was I, and elate
     When it was done.

The convent stood upon a hill;
  You could see far on either side;
The brothers had some fields to till,
  And they had forests far and wide.
     They taught my son to serve,
     And also how to pray.
I watched him often with the herd,
     Pass by that way.

One day there came an artist great;
  He was to paint the convent church.
Alas! it was my poor boy's fate
  To wait upon him in the church;
    He handed him his paint,
    And did I know not what.
It smelt so bad, he felt quite faint,
    And rued his lot.

Yet I must say he painted well;
  The saints alone would bring him fame.
My boy had something new to tell
  And show me every time I came.
    Oh, give me peace, I said,
    Such things are not for you.
Go lead the life that you have led,
    In that be true.

He answered nothing, but I saw
  He thought the more, though he was still.
I mocked him that he wished to draw,
  And told him then his father's will,
    That he should learn a trade,
    Thereby to win his bread,
Since he for hard work was not made,
    Every one said.

That night he kissed me when I went,
  He begged my blessing on his head;
He said that he had never meant
  To grieve me by the words he said;
    And I was glad to hear
    Such words from him at last,
For I had always had a fear
    His dream would last.

To make a long, long story short,
  My boy fled from his convent cell;
But he was one of the right sort,
  And learned to draw both quick and well.
    He made himself a way,
    Far off in the great town—
He slept, indeed, I heard them say,
    On eider down.

I often wondered that my lad
  Lived in such wealth, and sent me naught.
His father said that he was bad,
    'Twas only for himself he wrought;
      And so years passed away;
      My poor eyes they grew dim.
At length there came a knock one day,
      And it was him.

My God! and was that then my son,
    That skeleton, that scarce could walk!
One say at once his life was done,
    He hardly had the strength to talk.
      We bore him to his bed,
      And I sat by his side,
And every word was kind we said,
      Until he died.

It seemed that it was all a lie,
  About that wealth they said he had;
He lived up in a garret high,
  And starved himself to death, my lad.
      He won the prize, you say,
      The greatest prize they give.
What care I for the words they say,
      Or things they give?

Not long ago they came to look
  Upon the house where he was born;
On all the things that he forsook
  To go and lead that life forlorn.
      One said, " He asked for aid
      And I refused him then."
Another said, " Would I had staid,
      Up in his den."

They told me that my boy was great,
  I could be proud of such a son;
And they lamented much his fate
  And sorrowed that his life was done.
      And wherefor did he die?
      Alas! you know too well.
Neglect and want, the reason why,
      'Tis sad to tell.

No hand was stretched to help my boy,
   What care I what stands o'er his grave
Your monuments bring me no joy,
   Nor can they now, my poor boy save.
      Amidst the angel band
      Beyond the troubled sea,
My wayward youngest born now stands,
      And waits for me.

THE BOHEMIAN MONK.

I have steeped my soul in knowledge,
  Till my weary heart is faint;
And I sit now in my chamber
  Gazing sadly at the Saint,
At the Saint whose name I bear,
With the halo round his hair.

Does he look upon me wondering,
  That I bartered life for fame.
He, the preacher to the Gentiles,
  Would he have me do the same?
Hush, wild thoughts, for I am old,
And my weary heart is cold.

In my youth I yearned for knowledge,
  And I quaffed with burning lips
All the learning that the convent
  Gives its students in small sips.
Then I went to college old,
And my youth for knowledge sold.

Yes, fame came with laurels crowning
  This poor head of mine in youth;
And my name was held in honor,
  For my words were words of truth,
And my convent cell was sought
For the learning that I taught.

Was it wrong to yearn for knowledge?
　Knowledge that must pass away—
Sometimes as I sit and ponder,
　I can see another way,
To a glory without end,
Never yet by mortal penned.

Sometimes as I sit and think
　Of the days of long ago,
I can see the martyrs kneeling
　To receive the fatal blow;
And I almost seem to hear
Angels calling, " Have no fear."

And I look around my chamber,
　Stored with books and parchments rare;
And my heart is sick of knowledge,
　And I wish that I was there,
Where earth's thirst is quenched for aye,
And night turns to endless day.

Oh, my master, midst my learning
　Seldom I have thought of Thee;
And I taught my students knowledge,
　But I never spoke of Thee.
Now I dread to hear Thee say,
" Slothful servant, go away."

Oh, my master, in Thy mercy
　Spare me yet another year;
Let me speak in words undying
　To the youths who come to hear.
Give me strength to warn and guide
These few striplings to Thy side.

And if one of them should hearing,
　Yearn for that high crown of life
Which I missed with all my learning,
　Oh, God, fit him for the strife,
And then take me weary, old,
Where Thy face I can behold.

FAREWELL.

Before my charger bears me to the battle,
Upon the Elba plain,
I come again to see thee, dearest,
And 'neath thy chamber window, sweetest,
Plant a snowball bush by the same.

Should it in early spring be green with leaflets,
And many blossoms fair,
Think of me, then, oh my precious one,
Riding home, and the battle well won,
To you, the fairest of the fair.

But should the stem in spring be dried and leafless,
Without bud or flower,
Think of me, then, in some far-off plain,
By the enemy's swords lying slain—
And that I blessed thee in that hour.

THE WAY IS LONG.

Very long the footpath, hedged on either side,
As I trod it sadly. " Friends, farewell," I cried.
Farewell I have said now, unto all I love,
Hamlet of my parents, " Farewell, with my love."

Ah, where are the hours of my happy youth?
A thousand pities, they have passed forsooth!
Fate returns us nothing that she takes away,
Only this, she brings us pain and grief each day.

Mother sleeps in graveyard, father by her lies,
Will the dawn of Heaven bring them to my eyes?
When my heart thinks of them, sorrowful I say,
Will the grave bring me what life took away?

POEM V.—SONG.

On our cottage roof lies snow,
　Frozen snow to-day;
And beneath my mother lies,
　Fading fast away.

In the spring, when the snow melts
　In the garden near,
On my mother's grave the wind
　Wakes the grass, I fear.

I USED TO THINK.

Oft I used to think of far-reaching lanes,
Of flowery banks, and palmy plains.

Of lonely lion in his kingdom vast,
Of ruined cities, and of all the past.

Of mountain ranges, of the ocean's swell,
Of golden castles, crystal sea as well.

But now, oh God, I think of nothing more,
But of the darling, and the love I bore.

Now I only think, in cold and in snow,
If you lonely feel in your mound so low?

If you lonely feel in your coffin narrow,
Metal bound and strong, but oh so narrow?

And I think perhaps my little one sees me,
And my heart is faint, and my tears fall free.

And I think, yes day and night, I ponder—
Fearest thou in thy white shroud, over yonder?

Then the thought comes o'er me, thou wilt take me,
As I took thee in my arms, and hushed thee

When you used to cry, and my soul grows weak,
And my heart weeps for the child it would seek.

And I think that after this sad sorrow,
I shall clasp thee in the great to-morrow.

THE WEDDING.

She stands near to the altar—
Her eyes are filled with tears.
The old priest weds the stripling
Unto the girl she fears.

Draw her kerchief low, I pray—
Hide her red eyes weeping;
Sobbing as if heart should break,
She looks on his wedding.

Wrap a garment round her head—
Head that ached so madly.
Ah, alas! they bear her forth,
From the wedding sadly.

SONG X.

Calm have grown now our hearts,
  Very calm and still, my God.
Never think we of the past,
  What we were, and used to laud.

If we thought our hearts would ache,
  And despair would crown our brow;
Of the men we might have been,
  And the beings we are now.

THE FOREST NYMPH.

" Wander not in the dark forest,
    Where a woman roams at will,
And that woman is a wood nymph,
    Charming hearts to every ill."

" Charming hearts? With what, my mother?"
    " With her eyes of tenderest blue—
But a little while it lasteth—
    But a day, and then they rue.

" Treacherous is that nymph of forest,
    Many youths hath led astray;
Many she has left heart-broken,
    Many she has killed away."

" And where wanders she, my mother?"
    " By a rock, near fir trees tall.
She is queen of all the wood nymphs,
    And the forest hidden thrall.

" When the moon at full is shining,
    On the trees and creeping things,
She goes wandering in the forest,
    And a wondrous song she sings.

" Wander not in the dark forest,
    Where a woman roams at will,
And this woman is a wood nymph,
    Charming hearts to every ill."

The day is passed, night draweth near,
    He kissed his mother softly,
" Good-night," he said, " may Heaven send
    A dream most fair and lovely."

The night advanced, the moon came forth,
   Upon his bed he watched her.
He thought upon the lovely nymph,
   He longed to go and see her.

The moon rose high its silvery sheen,
   Danced in the forest's gloom;
And every dark twig beckoned now,
   And called him to his doom.

The youth sat up—he quickly thought—
   Too quickly—then arose,
With hasty care he clothed himself
   With his best Sunday clothes.

He smoothed his coat, then slipped behind
   The cottage, walking quickly.
He reached the rock, with fir trees dark,
   That looked down wickedly.

Upon a rock, beneath a fir,
   The forest nymph is singing.
The youth came quickly to her side,
   In her blue eyes he's gazing.

Oh, those blue eyes, so soft and fair—
   Entice the poor boy's passion;
His heart throbs with his new-born love,
   In an unwonted fashion.

Before she ended all was lost—
   He clasped her in his arms;
The forest trees looked darkly down,
   The moon shone with her charms.

They kissed each other many times,
   And then the nymph said slowly,
"Promise me, youth, no other lips
   You'll kiss, however holy?"

He promised—and went home at last,
   But sleep had fled away.
The moon grew pale, his mother rose,
   He too, rose up that day.

" But why so pale and wan, my son—
 Say, have you any pain?"   ·
" I could not sleep the whole night long,
 For the moonlight shining plain."

And when his mother slept in peoae,
 And all the stars were shining,
The youth beheld her once again,
 Amidst the pine trees sighing.

He saw the woman—heard her song,
 Resound in forest lonely.
Before the youth she glided on,
 He followed somewhat slowly.

He followed, followed on her steps—
 A precipice is yawning—
She glides before—he steps behind—
 Alas! love and its longing!

In the dark field, beneath the rock,
 On moss the youth lies sleeping,
On high the pale moon casts her light
 On the dead face, past weeping.

At home his mother sorrows sad;
 The wood nymph killed her son.
Because he kissed his mother dear,
 The poor youth's days were done.

GRASS.

Not beyond the ocean,
  Not beyond the hill.
Only a tuft of grass
  Grows between us still.
Beyond the hill birds fly,
  Winds blow o'er the sea.
But still that tuft of grass
  Grows 'twixt you and me.

Domou p. 310

SONG XX.

You ask how I would like to die?
Toward evening in the month of May,
Where dancing shadows love to play,
In jessamine bower, where harebells sway,
On some fair day, I'd pass away.

You ask how I would like to die?
Where blue forget-me-nots are seen,
And perfumed roses, purple sheen,
Would play on lips and breast, I ween,
When my sick heart should end its dream.

MYRTLE.

Plant a slip of myrtle green,
   Plant a slip, my maiden;
For your wedding it will be,
   For a wreath, my maiden.

When she planted it with joy,
   To the war he had to go;
And before the myrtle bloomed,
   Ah, she was lying low.

When he came back from the war,
   Myrtles they were seeking.
From her tree they cut a twig,
   For his coffin weeping.

MATER DOLOROSA.

I wander from the cloister,
  Adown the valley green.
The spring air wakes my fancies,
  The dreams that might have been.

The picture of God's mother,
  Hangs from the linden tree.
My soul it starts with memories—
  Forgotten dreams I see.

Ah, strange this picture hidden,
  Half hid by flowrets fair,
Was hung there by my mother,
  Years, years ago, just there.

Not long ago I gazing,
  Upon the picture felt
Within my soul a sorrow—
  A bitterness there dwelt.

And while I look it changes;
  My mother's face I see.
The features calm in prayer—
  That prayer is for me.

The eyes with tear-drops heavy,
  The lips drawn for a kiss;
My mother's face the last time
  She kissed my brow in bliss.

And back I wander slowly,
  Beneath the trees alone,
While thoughts of spring and sweetness,
  My God, from me have flown.

MYRTLE CYPRESS.

Oh happy we! Our highest wish fulfilled!
The myrtle thine—the cypress I have willed.

Who wished the sun, will ere the battle wane,
Be glad of moon and stars, to ease his pain.

The myrtle take, the cypress leave for me—
Whose fault is it, in graveyards it grows free.

Perhaps its branches singing in the air,
Peace to thy soul will bring, and dreams most fair.

Then will that grave of mine with roses bloom.
Be thou but happy, happy in thy doom.

FLAX.

All day long,
My wheel strong,
  Drives the flaxen thread along.
From the linen what will be?
He who waits will surely see—
  A shirt as white as lily.

Weaver mine,
Take this twine,
  Weave it quickly, weaver mine.
Linen thin, and soft and white;
Maiden shirts, for my delight—
  For his mother, see, a shroud.

THE OLD BACHELOR.

If I only had a wife,
  Surely I'd drink water.
In a beer room, by my life,
  Never I would saunter.

If I only had a wife,
  I'd go home at evening;
Not a friend, and not a strife,
  Then would stop my leaving.

If I only had a wife,
  A simple forest thrush,
I would sing, and I would fife,
  At home, till she said, "Hush."

If I only had a wife,
  Were she little and wee,
I'd stay by her, by my life,
  And ne'er go on a spree.

BATTLE.

Two hundred thousand men stand like a rock,
While two hundred thousand rush to the shock.

Two hundred thousand brains throb like fire,
Which will storm the hill? meet the lightning's ire?

Four hundred thousand lips mutter an oath—
With wolf's eyes they glare, carnage nothing loath.

Between two hills, the vale is filled with mist,
A smiling king stands on each hill, I wist.

With sidelong look they watch each other's face,
And speed " Good-morning " to each other's place.

Frowns on their brows—hate lurking in their eyes,
'Neath purple robes are hid hands white and wise.

Two kings upon two hills, their palms spread out,
Four hundred thousand men rush with a shout.

Ten thousand souls shriek out in mortal pain,
The kings applaud the music, " Call again."

Thousands of dying men at eve lie low,
The kings gaze as at an opera show.

A hundred thousand men rush in wild flight,
One of the kings says smiling, " A fine sight."

One king smiles and sets his throne higher,
The other bows low before the slyer.

Thousands lying, dying on the heather—
The two kings and generals drink together.

PILGRIM.

On my hat a feather,
  In my hand a staff,
I have wandered slowly,
  The world's better half.

Far away from your heart,
  Far and far away,
When I could not think, heart,
  Then I sang all day.

On my hat a feather,
  In my heart a pain,
I have wandered slowly,
  O'er and o'er the plain.

But at length I turned me,
  Once more to the past.
Useless to forget thee—
  Heart, I came at last.

VIOLETS BLOOM IN SPRING.

The violets flower in spring,
  And the heath in autumn gray.
Too late to love to-morrow,
  If you have not loved to-day.
    The world is full of maidens,
      Like poppies, blooming free.
    If one of them was mine,
      How happy I would be!

I'd give her half my homestead,
  And many a silver dime,
But roses prick the bachelor,
  That would pluck them out of time.
    For violets flower in spring,
      And the heath in autumn gray;
    I mocked the girls in my youth,
      They laugh at me to-day.

Domcu p 263

WHEN THE DAY ENDS.

When the day ends, and I shall sleep,
Come see my grave, but do not weep,
Nor let your grief be over wild.
    Who sleeps, is glad to rest in peace,
And holy is the evening mild,
    When the day ends.

I loved you and you know it well,
How much you helped me, can I tell?
How many pains and tears you dried—
    Then come and softly say, "You sleep,
But we shall meet somewhere at last,
    Because we loved."

ACH, NO—THOU SLEEPEST.

It seems to me, that in the spring's sweet air,
  Thy childish voice I almost seem to hear,
So far away—so far up in the air—
  From where the lark up in the vaulted sphere
Sings, and my heart goes out to meet thee there—
    Ach, no—thou sleepest!

It seems to me, when I kneel by thy mound
  Crossing myself, with folded hands I pray,
Thou nestles to my sorrowing heart, and round
  Thy presence lingers as it used to stay,
And in thy eyes I gaze without a sound—
    Ach, no—thou sleepest.

CONCORD IN THE NATION.*

Concord, brothers! Stand by our mother—
  Our mighty mother—our only love.
And let the light of our glorious past
  Shine on the lion flag from above.
Long sleep has made us once more strong,
  The future will us honor yield.
Only concord, concord, brothers,
  Shield us, St. Václav, with thy shield.†

Ah, once the sun of glory shining,
  Illustrious made Bohemia's name.
From the Baltic to the Adriatic,
  Our native land was known to fame.
The sun shone, and our land was great,
  From mountain top to fruitful field.
Only concord, concord, brothers,
  Shield us, St. Václav, with thy shield.

Bohemia spake, and the world trembled—
  From far and wide they quaking heard.
She raised her voice to God, and heaven,
  By holy song of hers, was stirred.
It was Bohemia's voice that sang,
  The truth that from her mountains pealed.
Only concord, concord, brothers,
  Shield us, St. Václav, with thy shield. ·

Oh, for the true words, and the true faith,
  Of our Cyril and Methodej.
Bohemia on the bloody mountains
  Lost their freedom through faith in you.

---

* This poem received the poetic prize in Prague.

† St. Václav (Wenzel), patron saint of Bohemia, was murdered
by his brother, a heathen, in a church. He was king of Bohemia,
A.D. 928. Murdered by Boleslav.

Knock, oh, Bohemians! on your hills,
 There sleep the brave who would not yield.
Only concord, concord, brothers,
 Shield us, St. Václav, with thy shield.

Yes, there is honor in a downfall
 After a most desperate warfare.
When the land lies crushed, but not conquered—
 For the free soul still lingers there.
Like the phœnix from dead ashes,
 Warriors arise from our fields.
Only concord, concord, brothers,
 Shield us, St. Václav, with thy shield.

My country, my poor blinded country—
 What fate now can cause thee to blaze?
You see not the blood that is streaming,
 To springs of the far-away days.
It blazes the blood on our hills—
 It calls us never to yield.
Only concord, concord; brothers,
 Shield us, St. Václav, with thy shield.

The bones of our fathers are scattered—
 Their blood it is chill now in death.
From their bones will rise up the giants,
 Their blood is the red morning's breath.
The red clouds call us to glory,
 They smile on us never to yield.
Only concord, concord, brothers,
 Shield us, St. Václav, with thy shield.

With concord—then on to the battle,
 The east is ablaze—and I dream,
I hope that the hour is nearing,
 When the God of nations will seem
To call us once more unto fame,
 Once more to the honorable field.
Only concord, concord, brothers,
 Shield us, St. Václav, with thy shield.

MOUNTAIN BALLAD.

" Tell me, granny, granny dearest, what will heal a
    wound,
    Heal the cut of one sore wounded, that he will not
      die?"
" Open wounds on human bodies are not easily closed,
    Only the juice of witches' herb heals beneath the
      sky."
" Tell me, granny, granny dearest, what will ease the
    pain,
    Heal the pain of one sore tortured, wounds on head
      and brow?"
For such wounds on brow 'and forehead, there is but
    one aid,
    Leaves of the forest strawberry, laid on aching
      brow.

The little child in haste went to the neighbor's pas-
    ture,
" Oh, give me of thy juice, witches' herb, that heals all
    pain."
Then from the meadow to the forest's shade she
    wandered,
" Oh, strawberry of God, give me of thy leaves that
    heal all pain."
All that she wanted, see, the flowers gave her gladly,
    And to the church she ran, where Christ before the
      altar,
Outstretched upon the cross of shame, bows his dying
    head.
" On Thy holy side, Jesus mine, I will not falter,
    But lay the healing herbs on Thy side and bloody
      brow,
    Then all the pain will cease from Thy side and
    wounded brow.

In the church steeple, lo! the bells are rung clear,
And many people came from far and near;
For what the little child had wished to do,
God had fulfilled, the wounds were closed anew.

In that mountain village still they show the picture.
Healed are the wounds of the crucified one, and in-
    stead
Of the crown of thorns are lilies that droop o'er the
    dead.

SADDLE MY CHARGER.

" Like the wild storm, I would fly through the air—
Saddle my horse! In the forest I'll dare! "
    " Lady, my lady! the rocks seem to shake,
     While the heavens with lightning are flaming,
     In the storm the forest moans like a lake—
Oh, go not my lady—'Tis awful to-day! "

" With lightning and wind I'll ride for a stake!
Go saddle my charger—make no mistake."
    " Lady, my lady! Oh, risk not your life,
     Wild beasts in the forest prowl to-night,
     And foxes are howling amidst the strife,
Who knows if the forest you'd leave alive?"

' To hunt the wild beasts in storm is delight,
Saddle! The fox with my spear I'll kill outright! "
    " Lady, oh listen! Your lord comes to-day—
     Will you not welcome him back to his home?
     You know he'll repay you—revenge his way!
Stay at home lady! Dreadful is your lord!"

" I know it! Him only I dread to-day—
With the whirlwind I'll fly out of his way!
     Terrible is it to live in his sight.
     Awful to meet him, no love in my heart—
     Saddle! Let me hide myself from his might!
With whirlwind and foxes 'tis easier to fight."

THE SPINNING GIRL.

" What are you spinning, my sister, day by day,
  That your tears fall on the soft flax in this way? "

" My tears they fall with grief, o'er my love's short
    dream!
  What I spin? Why my wedding garment I ween."

" What spin you at night—that no dreams make you
    doze,
  When no wedding you'll have, sister mine, these days?"

" No bridal I'll have, but my lover will wed,
  To his wedding I'll go in white dress, I have said."

" What spin you in haste, by the moon's pale ray?
  Does your lover haste to the altar, I say? "

" I must hasten, my brother, the time is near—
  In my shroud I am spinning the moonlight drear."

The bells are tolling reproachfully and slow—
To her grave they bear the spinner, lying low.

Why are the bells pealing, so gladsome and clear,
For a wedding they ring, with their noisy cheer.

But at night when the lovers are kissing sweet,
At midnight the dead rise in their winding sheet.

" My bride, oh, who is it, that comes to us see? "
" 'Tis the moon—there is no one but you and me."

" Who kisses my forehead? Whose tears on my cheek?"
" The dew of evening, or perhaps the moon freak."

" No, 'tis my dead bride! See in the midnight cold,
Her dress in the moonlight shines fold upon fold.

" She waves me a farewell, adieu seems to say,
Then beckons me onward to follow her way.

" I follow! By power of witchcraft drawn on!"
" My lover! What madness is this, strange and strong."

He climbs through the window, and stands on the
sill,
" Keep hold! Now alone God can save if He will!"

The moonlight is drawing him—dizzy the height—
Life's burden has passed from him into the night

" Stop lover! One step and death stands in your way!"
Where he stood, falls undimmed the moonlight's
ray.

The moonlight shines clear on the river's white bed,
Where he and the spinner united lie dead.

FORSAKEN.

Weep, my maiden, weep and cry,
  To your lover say farewell.
To the only one you love—
  He who in your heart doth dwell.

Drafted in the warrior band,
  Far away he'll have to serve.
May be, in the living land,
  You will see his face no more.

Oh, that I were in my grave,
  Deep beneath the emerald grass,
O'er my mound a heavy cross,
  Pressing my poor head, alas!

Then two eyes would only weep,
  Where four now are bathed in tears;
Then two eyes would only burn
  With the scalding, bitter tears.

SMITH'S SONG.

No man greater than a blacksmith,
Honest, sturdy is the blacksmith;
Firm upon his feet he standeth,
　Dealing heavy blow on blow.
With quick hand his axe he handeth,
　Many works before him grow.
　　　And so, and so,
　　　Blow upon blow,
Like thunder they fall on the anvil, and lo!
He misses the iron by never a blow.

Blacksmiths, like all things in keeping,
Heavy blows, and not much speaking,
Manly speech and diligent work,
　Heart for every noble thing.
And so we hear him at his work,
　Dealing blows that loudly ring,
　　　And so, and so,
　　　Blow upon blow,
Like thunder they fall on the anvil, and lo!
He misses the iron by never a blow.

The blacksmith is a man of truth,
At home, or in the world, forsooth.
The crooked he makes straight, the bad
　He throws away in the dark.
A lover of the law, not sad,
　He deals his heavy blows, hark!
　　　And so, and so.
　　　Blow upon blow,
Like thunder they fall on the anvil, and lo!
He misses the iron by never a blow.

The blacksmith is a friend of toil,
He waits his time in the turmoil.
Until the iron has turned red,
  Then lets the blow fall quickly.
A thorough Check,* without a dread,
  A smith, and not one sickly.
      And so, and so,
      Blow upon blow,
Like thunder they fall on the anvil, and lo!
He misses the iron by never a blow.

Bohemia is our native land,
And blessed of God, with coal our land;
The coal it gives us light and heat,
  And the iron makes us strong.
Strong hands can do great deeds, and meet
  For a heart that knows no wrong.
      And so, and so,
      Blow upon blow,
Like thunder they fall on the anvil, and lo!
He misses the iron by never a blow.

Bohemians have been blacksmiths bold,
Strong of arm, they have kept their hold,
Made plows, and harrows, thrashing frail,
  Axe and hammer, bar and nail.
With shame their cheeks were never pale—
  They knew not such a word as fail.
      And so, and so,
      Blow upon blow,
Like thunder they fall on the anvil, and lo!
They miss the iron by never a blow.

---

* The Bohemians call themselves Checks.

THE STRANGE GUEST.

Mirth and dancing, music playing,
    Song and jest alone are heard;
And the bride with joy is laughing
    At the bridegroom's generous cheer.

" Listen, servants! men and women! "
    Cries the bridegroom, wild with joy.
" Open pantry, open cellars—
    Eat and drink without alloy."

Mirth and dancing, by a table
    Sits an unknown guest and cries:
" Hoj! for one dance with that maiden,
    Life I'd give, like him who dies."

Once they danced around the chamber,
    Lo, the smile died on her face.
Twice they danced and pale her features,
    Pale like snow in that wild pace.

" Ho! Art pale indeed, my loved one!
    Does thy memory start with pain?
Is it hard to see thy Zdenko,
    On thy wedding day again?"

On the third round they have entered—
    In her ear he whispers low;
Senseless from his clasp she swooneth,
    In the bridegroom's arms falls slow.

Cries and amazement—music stops—
  They all rush to help the bride.
Where is the man?   The unknown guest!
  Away!   Dark is the night to hide!

The music plays—the dance has ceased,
  All joy has now passed for aye.
To endless rest they bore the bride,
  In the dance she passed away.

CHRISTMAS EVE.
PART FIRST.

Darkness like the grave; on the window frost,
　But in the room beside the stove is warm.
By the fire's blaze granny sits and nods,
　While the maidens spin the soft flax by storm.

Spin around, whirl around, spinning-wheel mine,
Advent is nearing, and rest shall be thine,
For soon, for oh soon will be Christmas time.

Oh, diligent maidens I love to see
　Spinning their flax in the long winter night,
For pay they'll receive when spinning is done;
　And a linen pile is a gladsome sight.

And youths will come for a diligent girl,
　They will say, " Oh, maiden, beloved, be mine!
I will take thee home as my cherished wife,
　And I will be wholly, wholly thine.

" I'll be thy husband, and thou'lt be my wife, .
　Give me thy hand, that I know it is so!"
Then the maiden will cut her linen fine,
　And gladly her wedding shirts she will sew.

Spin around, whirl around, spinning wheel mine,
Advent is nearing and rest will be thine;
For soon, for oh soon will be Christmas time. .

PART SECOND.

Ho! thou Christmas evening,
　Filled with mystic awe.
Good perhaps thou bringest,
　Better then we saw.

For the farmer fodder,
    That his cows grow sleek.
For the fowls some barley,
    Peas then let them seek.

For the fruit trees compost,
    Made of pounded bones.
For the one who fasteth,
    Lights from other zones.

I, an honest maiden,
    With my heart still free,
Fain would see the lover
    That will come for me.

Far behind the forest,
    Near the little bridge,
Stands a willow ancient,
    Snow on tree and ridge.

Willow stooping downward,
    Leaning on the ice,
Drooping where the blue sea
    Now has turned to ice.

Here they say that maidens,
    In the moonlight clear,
May behold their lover,
    If they have no fear.

I, who fear no evil,
    Will break through the ice.
With an axe I'll cut it,
    Gaze down in the ice.

Deep, deep down they tell me,
    In the frozen sea,
I shall see my future,
    If I do not flee.

PART THIRD.

Mary and Hannah, two beautiful girls,
  That bloom like the roses in spring.
And which the fairest, oh nobody knows,
  They are flowers that bloom in spring.

Should she speak to a youth, gentle and soft,
  In fire he'd spring for her sake.
Should the other smile, forgotten the first,
  Forgotten the first for her sake.

Midnight is near, and the night it is dark;
  But the wee stars are shining bright.
They shine round the moon, like sheep round the
    crook
  Of shepherd that watches by night.

Midnight is near, 'tis the mystical night,
  The night when our Saviour was born.
On the new-fallen snow footsteps are seen,
  They lead to the willow forlorn.

Down on her knees the maiden is gazing—
  The other one stands by her side.
" Hannah, dear Hannah, oh gold heart, now say,
  What is it the future can hide?"

" I see a cottage—but all in a mist—
  Like the one Veník * is building.
The mist is clearing—oh, now I see clear,
  A door, and some one near standing.

" His coat is dark green—yes, green is his coat,
  His hat on one side—now I see;
The flowers I gave him, stuck on one side,
  My God! 'tis my Veník I see."

---

* Veník (Václav) Wenzel.

She jumped to her feet, her heart beating wild,
   The other one knelt on the ice.
" God give, Mary dear, you also behold,
   Your happiness down in the ice."

" Oh, I see, I see, but all is gloomy,
   Shrouded in some darkness dreary,
Faint red lights, from out the darkness,
   Light the church's altar dreary.

" Something dark amidst white dresses fluttering—
   Now the mist is growing clear, I see—
*Bridesmaids, but, oh God, they follow something;
   Cross and coffin all I see!"

PART FOURTH.

Summer winds are softly blowing,
   On the scented new-mown hay.
Fields and garden full of flowers,
   Promising a harvest day.
From the church one heard the singing,
And the wedding music ringing,
   As they led the happy pair.

Stately bridegroom, tall and stalwart,
   Walking midst the wedding guests.
Green the coat upon his shoulders,
   And his hat on one side rests.
As she saw him in the midnight,
Now she sees him in the daylight,
   As he leads her to his home.

Summer's past.   Cold winds are blowing
   O'er the dreary harvest fields.
Bells are tolling as they carry
   One who now no longer feels.

---

* In Bohemia when a young girl or lad dies, they are followed
to their grave by bridesmaids or grooms; the richer the dead
the larger the number; the girls wear wreaths of myrtle and are
dressed in white.

Bridesmaids with wax candles follow,
Weeping—music sad and hollow,
  Sung in accents cold and clear,
  " Misserere, sleep in peace!"

" Who with myrtle wreath is sleeping,
  In the coffin's narrow space?"
Dead, oh dead, and past all weeping—
  Fairest lily of her race,
Blooming like a cherished flower,
Till cut in an evil hour,
  Poor, poor, beautiful Mary!

PART FIFTH.

Terrible cold! on the window is frost,
  But in the room beside the stove, is warm.
By the fire's blaze granny sits and nods,
  And again the maidens spin through the storm.

Spin around, whirl around, spinning wheel mine,
  Advent is nearing, and rest will be thine.
For soon, for oh soon will be Christmas time.

Ah, thou Christmas evening,
  Filled with mystic awe,
When I think upon thee,
  My heart beats with awe.

We were sitting spinning,
  As we sit to-day,
But a year has rolled by—
  Two have gone away.

One is sitting sewing,
  Baby shirts I ween.
Three months Mary sleepest,
  In the graveyard green.

We were sitting spinning,
  As we sit to-day.
Ere the year be finished,
  Will we meet, I say?

Spin around, whirl around, spinning wheel mine,
Man's life is a dream, and a trying time,
And life is a puzzle hard to divine.

Oh, better to live hoping,
　And our future not to see,
Than to know what will befall,
　When we cannot, cannot flee.

THE RETURN.

Oh, the peaceful, quiet village, nestling midst the
    Bohemian hills,
  With its humble straw-thatched hamlets clustering
    round the little church.
On one side the great lake stretches, fed by many bright
    mountain rills,
  On the other side are forests, pine and cedar, silvery
    birch.

I can see it all before me, as I left it in my boyhood;
  Left my parents, left my village, to go soldiering in
    the world.
Fifty years have come and faded—still the cross stands
    where it stood,
  Only I am changed and weary, strange that this was
    once my world.

And now I come back with honors, with my medals,
    with all my fame,
  Just to look upon the village where my happy boy-
    hood strayed,
Just to seek out in the little churchyard the few graves
    that bear my name,
  And to say a humble prayer where my parents low
    are laid.

Yes, I left them in my boyhood, careless of their bitter
    anguish—
  And the warnings of my mother entered not my heed-
    less ears,
Till years after, I lay wounded far from home in bitter
    anguish,
  Then I felt my parent's sorrow, then I realized their
    fears.

But with strength came happier feelings, and soon my
    soldier's heart beat high,
  When I heard I was promoted, and a medal graced
    my breast.
Still the war raged on unending, many a comrade saw I
    die,
  While I rose and rose in station, with more medals
    on my breast.

And their letters came so seldom, telling of their
    homely pastimes;
  Of the endless toil and trouble that weigh down the
    peasant heart,
That it struck me with strange new wonder, like some
    old forgotten chime
  Wafted to us in our labor from the far-off ancient
    mart.

And the years passed on so quickly 'neath the tender
    southern sunlight,
  I forgot to count how many since I saw my native
    land;
And the past seemed strange and dreary—dim and un-
    real to my sight,
  When I paused to watch the peasants cutting vines
    with skillful hand.

True, they wrote to me in longing, begging I would
    come and see them,
  Saying they were old and weary, and would see their
    soldier boy,
But there always came a reason why I could not go and
    see them,
  Could not clasp them to my bosom in the rapture of
    my joy.

So the years pass'd, I rose higher—until a general's
    rank was mine,
  Then I asked to be permitted to send in my own dis-
    charge,
Pleading that my health was too feeble to serve longer
    in the line,
  Pleading I had wounds in plenty, and now longed to
    be discharged.

While I waited for the answer, came a letter with sad
tidings,
Telling me my poor old father had been stricken down
by death.
Yes, a tree had fallen on him, and the unexpected tidings,
Coming sudden on my mother, had deprived her of her
life.

Long, they told me, she lay dying, half unconscious,
praying slowly,
For her son who was a soldier, for her boy who was
away,
Saying, " Could I see him only, oh, my Father, just
and holy;
Could he close my eyes in slumber, happy were my
dying day."

Oh, my God, she never saw me, never heard my piteous
weeping;
Never saw me with my medals pass the threshold of
the door;
Now her soldier boy stands sighing by the grave where
she is sleeping,
Thinking of the many sorrows that so patiently she
bore.

Thinking of my poor old father I had left half broken-
hearted,
Of the little baby sister, now an angel up on high,
And the changes in my brothers and my sisters since
we parted,
And I almost feel that gladly I would lay me down
and die.

Farewell, then, my native village, and the hamlet where
I was born,
Fifty years ago I left you in the hope of winning
fame,
And I leave you now, forever, famous, crippled, and
most forlorn,
Having spent my life's best hours just to win a glori-
ous name.

LEGEND OF THE LADY IN WHITE.*

The whirlwind is howling—the night it is dark—
The mountains like giants frown down on the scene.
The hall from whose windows a flickering light shines,
Is the only shelter for miles to be seen.
The whirlwind is raging through turrets and eaves,
It shrieks by the windows, it howls at the door.
Near by in the forest the trees creak and moan,
As the wind rushes through, with terrible roar.
" God be with the stranger that wanders to-night,
Amidst our wild mountains," the servant said low,
And lit the red light at the Crucifix's feet.
" God bless us, and keep us, and save us from woe."
There's a knock at the door—the servant turns pale,
And crosses himself, ere he opens the gate.
Two strangers are standing, he sees their long robes,
And blesses himself, and the strangers that wait.
" In the name of the Lord, whose servants we are,
We beseech thee, shelter us but for to-night.
Our way we have lost, and the tempest is great,
Let us stay here, I pray thee, till the dawn's light."
The servant bows. " Reverend fathers," he said,

---

* This celebrated ghost is one of the most historical in Europe.
She was born 1430, baptized Bertha (Perchta), married Hans von
Licktenstein (of the steirischen Linie von Muran). She died in April,
1476, and was buried in Vienna in the vault to "den Shotten."
During the last part of her life she lived with her brother,
Heinrich von Neuhausen. There are still many of her letters
that can be seen and read, also letters from others who declare
that they saw her. She was seen in Berlin by the Burggrafen
von Zollern, also in Lyons, Paris, London, Stockholm and Co pen-
hagen, where members of the Rosenbergs (now princes of
Schwartzenberg) had wandered. Johann of the house of Liech-
tenstein, Domherr (canon or prebendary), was the last who saw
her. He is said to have made peace, with saying mass and join-
ing their hands. The same day next year he died.—*Chronik of
Böhmen*, Prague, 1852.

" Our master ne'er sent a poor monk from his door,
And though he is absent, I bid you come in,
Come in, worthy fathers, be fed from his store."
" God bless now thy master, his house and his field!
The Lord will reward him for what he has done;
Not a mouthful of food have we had to-day,
We were lost in the mountains and woods, my son."
The servant led on, and the monks came behind,
" Reverend fathers," he said, " the kitchen is warm;
Come sit by the fire, and eat to your fill—
'Tis better than straying without in the storm.
Were our master at home, you would sup in the hall,
But gladly we'll give you the best that we can."
" My son," said the monk, " we are easy to please,
Who follow the footsteps of ' The Son of Man.' "
They sit in the kitchen, one young and one old,
And eat of the food that the servants have brought.
The wind down the chimney howls dreary and wild,
Like the souls of the lost who evil have wrought.
" 'Tis a terrible night," said the wan old monk,
" It reminds me indeed of a night long past,
Of a terrible night when our Domherr died—
Ah, years ago in the beginning of fast.
The whirlwind was howling—the night it was dark.
I sat by his bed, and I counted my beads.
He knew he must die, for a ghost had appeared,
A ghost of his family in deep widow's weeds."
" A ghost, reverend father! and how could that be?"
" I know not, my children,' the legend is old,
And awful indeed, as the whirlwind to-night,
I can but relate you the tale I was told.

    The daughter of a noble line,
      In Neuhausen she saw the light,
    Where all her childish years were spent,
-    In innocent and pure delight.
    Beloved of all, with maiden grace,
      She grew up like a flower fair,
    And many were the youths who came,
      And praised her face, and praised her hair.
    On one alone her father smiled,
      A goodly youth, John Lichtenstein.
    And when she reached her nineteenth year,
      He told the youth, the girl is thine,

Ah, merry rang the wedding bells—
  And many were the guests that came,
And gathered round the festive board
  Were not a few of noble name.
The first few years they lived in peace,
  As well befits a married pair,
Then John of Lichtenstein grew cold,
  And left his wife to her despair.
The devil jealousy took room
  Within his heart, and he would fain
Have walled his wife within her room,
  So burning was his jealous pain.
They lived indeed a dreadful life,
  Which every day grew worse and worse.
He kept her like the meanest born,
  Without a home, without a purse.
For years she bore her wretched lot,
  And wifelike tried to smile through tears,
Till life became to her a hell,
  And death for her lost all its fears.
At length endurance had an end,
  Ill-treatment drove her from her home;
She left her lord, and fled at night,
  To her old childhood's home alone.
Her brother took her, eased her pain,
  And would have played the kinsman's part,
Made peace—or dueled with her lord,
  And stabbed him through his wicked heart,
But Bertha said, "Let him alone—
  God may forgive him, but not I.
Since I am safe with you at home,
  Oh, wherefore, brother, should he die?"
Long years she lived with him in peace,
  There where her childish feet had strayed,
Was mother to his orphaned brood,
  When he in his low grave was laid.
Her time she passed in works of love,
  The naked clothed, the poor one fed,
Was loved and honored through the land,
  And blessings fell upon her head,
So years passed on, her husband died;
  But unforgiving still, she said,
"God may forgive him, but not I.
  'Tis well indeed that he is dead."

At length she also fell asleep,
  Was buried with all solemn state;
But lo! her spirit found no rest,
  And very dreadful was her fate.
In the cold moonlight she was seen,
  Dressed in her bridal dress and veil,
Pacing the halls she knew in life,
  With features very calm and pale.
She came to one, she came to all,
  That had her blood within their veins;
She came at morn, she came at noon—
  They met her in familar lanes;
She gazed upon them with sad eyes,
  Then slowly faded from their sight;
Before their death she came in black,
  But otherwise was dressed in white.
In every castle of her race,
  Her sad white face was seen at times;
She followed them from place to place,
  And she was seen in many climes;
She stood beside the new-born babe,
  The dying gazed upon her face;
In vain were masses for her soul,
  Said by the righteous of her race.
In Neuhausen she made her home,
  If ghosts, indeed, a home can make,
And it was there her soul found rest,
  Found rest at length for Jesus' sake.
Our Domherr * was a righteous man,
  A godly priest who loved the truth;
But he was of her haunted race,
  And had to die for her, forsooth.
Once to Neuhausen he was called,
  And in a stately room was led,
Where many family paintings hung,
  There they had made for him a bed.
'Twas evening and the candle's light
  Half hid the portraits hanging low.
And one was of a wedded pair,
  It seemed to him he ought to know;

---

*Canon.

The bridegroom had a scowling look,
  The bride was very fair and pale;
Dressed in her bridal robes, she stood
  With myrtle wreath and long white veil.
Long time our Domherr stood and prayed
  Her tortured spirit might find rest;
Then laid him down to sleep in peace,
  With holy feelings in his breast.
At midnight, at the stroke of twelve,
  He woke up with a sudden fear;
The moonlight flooded all his room,
  And lo! poor Bertha's ghost was near.
He felt the blood rush to his heart,
  While horror numbed his very brain;
He could not move, he scarce could breathe,
  And so he laid there in his pain.
She stepped from out the portrait's frame,
  Her white dress glimmered in the light;
He saw her dark eyes on him rest,
  And almost fainted at the sight;
She came and stood beside his bed—
  He felt the coldness of the grave
Waft on him from her garments white,
  Then shrieked in horror, " Oh, Christ, save! "
And with the name of Christ all fear
  Was banished from our Domherr's soul.
" All righteous spirits praise the Lord,"
  He said.   " How can I ease thy dole?
Speak now, poor spirit, I entreat,
  Or sleep in peace within thy grave!
What unforgiven sins are thine,
  That maketh thee the devil's slave? "
" Alas! " she said, " Oh, kinsman, hear!
  I of my husband ever said,
God may forgive him, but not I;
  'Tis well, indeed, that he is dead.
I cannot enter Heaven's rest
  Till I have made my peace on earth.
Now thou wert chosen for this act,
  From the first hour of thy birth.
My husband, for the ill he wrought,
  In purgatorial pains must burn—

He also would be reconciled
  To ease his torments long and stern.
Long years we waited for this hour—
  If thou art willing, lo, we meet,
All three to-morrow, to make peace,
  Before God's holy mercy seat."
The Domherr said, " Oh, wretched pair, -
  Most gladly I will join your hands;
Come but to-morrow, as you say,
  And we will break the devil's bands."
The spirit faded from his sight—
  New horror filled his trembling fame.
What was this vision he had seen?
  And would his kindred come again?
All day he fasted, thought and prayed,
  And when the evening shadows came,
Built a high altar in his room,
  And knelt in prayer before the same.
Wax candles burnt before the shrine,
  And incense filled the heavy air,
When on the stroke of twelve o'clock,
  Before him stood the troubled pair.
" What will you? " asked the godly priest.
" We seek forgiveness," both they said;
And then our Domherr took their hands,
  And joined them as when they were wed.
The room was filled with heavenly light—
  An unseen chorus sang God's praise;
The Domherr and the wretched ones
  Acknowledged now God's wondrous ways;
By unknown hands were censers swung,
  The room was filled with perfume sweet,
All three fell down upon their knees
  In prayer before the mercy seat.
Angelic voices sang God's praise,
  So loud the castle rang with song.
The Domherr knelt before the shrine—
  He never knew himself how long—
At length a voice broke on his ear,
  The voice of one he knew so well.
" Oh, blessed kinsman, in a year,
  Thou too will come with us to dwell.

Who can repay what thou hast done,
  But He who chose you for His own.
This day a year hence I will come,
  To lead thee to the heavenly throne."
And it was so—in one short year.
  Our Domherr slept amidst the dead;
But ere he died, he told us all
  That Bertha stood beside his bed;
She held a palm branch in her hand,
  Her face was lit with heavenly light.
" I've come for thee," she softly said,
  " To lead thee to the Lord's delight."
Our Domherr smiled, and stretched his hand,
  " Oh, lead me to my Lord," he said.
A rapturous light shown on his face,
  And when it faded he was dead.

He ended.   The whirlwind raged on in the night,
It howled by the windows, it shrieked at the door,
The terrified servants with horror it filled,
The thought of the demon as never before;
The spiritual world with its weal and its woe,
Seemed near them; they trembled to think they might
      see
The form of some being no more of this world,
And seeing be powerless even to flee.
" Oh, father," they said, " 'tis a terrible tale,
And had you not told us, who would have believed?
Though all of us know the dead can arise,
They generally only the wicked deceive."
" My children," the monk said, " the living and dead
Are all in the hands of the Lord we adore.
Oh, pray that your sins be forgiven on earth,
Be nailed to the cross that our dear Saviour bore."
The servant now led them to where they might rest
And sleep, if they chose, till the coming of day,
And when the sun rose, and the storm had been stilled,
With blessings and thanks the two monks went their
      way.

SIMON ABELES.*

Here in this grave a little martyr lies—
A little boy who counted but ten years,
    Killed by his father in a moment dread.
    This Jewish child amidst the Christian dead,
Was carried by all Prague with groans and sighs,
In the Týn Minster amidst many tears.

Killed by his father! 'Tis an awful thought—
This Jewish boy had dared to be baptized,
    Had dared to tell his father of his hope,
    And bid defiance to the whip and rope
He knew would wait him for the faith he sought,
The faith that by his fathers was despised.

Oft when they drove him forth to earn his bread,
In the Týn Minster he had stood and heard
    The gracious message of our blessed Lord,
    And he in silence stood there and adored.
At length one day a Jesuit priest had said,
" What brings thee here to listen to the Word?"

And then the Jewish boy his heart outpoured,
Told of the love he felt for Him who died,
    And how he yearned to come within that fold
    Of perfect peace of which the priest had told.
The monk then told him, from his mind well stored,
Things of the faith, for which the poor boy sighed.

---

* Simon Abeles, a Jewish boy, was killed by his own father,
because he turned Christian, the 21st of February, 1694. He was
buried with great pomp as a martyr, in a glass coffin, on the right
side of the altar in the Týn Minster in Prague.—*Chronik von
Böhmen*, 1854.

And so they met and conversed many days,
Until the priest said one morn, "Come, my son,
   I will baptize thee, since it is thy will,
   But thou must come and see me often still."
"My father," said the child, "you know God's ways,
 - There must be struggle, ere the crown be won."

"Come live with us, my child," the monk replied,
"If aught you dread before your father's wrath."
   "My heart misgives me," said the boy. "I fear,
   I know not what—ah, well, the Lord is near."
And so they parted, and the poor boy sighed,
While the monk watched him going down the path.

Three days went by—the boy was seen no more—
Then the priests sought him, and they found him
    dead;
   Killed by his father in a moment wild,
   There on his bed they found the bleeding child,
With marks of many sufferings that he bore,
Before his childish spirit to Christ fled.

They hung his father. But the martyred boy
With solemn pomp they bore to his last rest.
   By the high altar amidst chanting sad,
   And grief of the vast multitude, the lad
Was buried, while they prayed that heaven's joy
Might be his own, who died a martyr blessed.

LEGEND OF THE STONE MAIDEN.*

" Do you hear the church-bells ringing,
    Ringing from the distant mart?
With their metal tongues they're singing,
" Give the Lord alone thy heart!"
Petronella, take thy mass book,
    It is time that we should start."

" Oh, no, granny, I am going
    Where the strawberries are ripe.
Midst the green leaves they are glowing
    Like a crimson velvet stripe;
In the forest there are flowers,
    Violets, and gipsies pipe."

" Oh, my child, are you lightheaded?
    Why to-day is St. John morn,
Think of him who was beheaded
    In his prison cell forlorn.
Be not like that wanton maiden—
    Better she was never born!"

" Oh, dear granny, she was skillful,
    And could dance with wondrous grace;
But St. John was very willful,
    And he did not know his place.
One should leave kings all their pleasures,
    And not blame them to their face."

---

* This legend is told in Tetschen, in the valley of the Kante, of a mountain that looks like a girl with a basket.—*Chronik von Böhmen*, Prague, 1852.

" Oh, thou God-forsaken creature!
    Wilt thou judge the saints in light?
Art thou then a better teacher
    Than the church that preaches right?
Wilt thou blame that blessed martyr,
    Who is now an angel bright?"

" I will wander in the sunlight,
    Gather berries all the day,
And to-night I'll dance till midnight,
    Spite of everything you say."
And the wicked girl went laughing,
    Laughing gladly on her way.

Then her granddame sadly weeping,
    Took her way unto the church,
Saying " Better thou went sleeping
    In the graveyard 'neath the birch,
Than to scorn the holy teachings,
    And to leave thy faith in lurch."

In the wood the wicked maiden
    Gathered berries ripe and red,
Then with basket heavy laden,
    Hid her where the two ways led;
When she saw her granddame coming,
    Hear the wicked words she said.

" Look, old crow, what comes of praying—
    Nothing but an empty sack.
I while in the sunlight straying
    Found of strawberries no lack;
Seems to me that in rewarding
    Your old saint is over slack."

" Wretched girl! That God would turn thee
    To a stone upon the way!
Dost thou revile St. John and me—
    And think to escape all pay?
An awful fate will be thine own—
    That is all I have to say."

Homeward went the granddame sadly,
   Thinking of that naughty maid,
Then she eat her dinner gladly,
   Wondering where the maiden stayed;
Sat her down and began nodding,
   Murmuring, " She is now afraid."

Soon the neighbors came in horror.
" Petronella's turned to stone!
Come and see her to thy sorrow,
   Standing on the hill alone;
Grown like a mighty mountain,
   With her basket turned to stone."

Pale with horror went the granddame,
   Gazed upon the far-off hill,
Then calling loud the Virgin's name,
   She fell in a death-cramp chill.
The neighbors bore her to her grave,
   And the mound they show you still.

By Tetschen is the mountain sere,
   And the peasants love to tell
To naughty maids who will not fear,
   The trouble that once befell
A girl who laughed at good St. John,
   And her grandmother as well.

A JEWISH LEGEND OF PRAGUE.*

They were dying, dying daily,
    The small children of the Jews;
And each mother's heart was heavy,
    As she heard the bitter news.
Every mother clasped her infant
    With a love unfelt before,
While she sought Jehovah's blessing
    For the little child she bore.
They were dying, dying daily,
    Still the little prattling tongue
That had been the household's treasure,
    And the little lips that sung,
Stilled in death the restless fingers,
    And the little toddling feet;
And their parents in their sorrow
    Had no comfort but to weep.
One by one Jehovah called them,
    Till a home was scarcely found
Where some loved one was not lying
    In the cold and noisome ground.
Prayer and fasting, naught availed them,
    Day by day the sickness spread;
Raging midst the Jewish children,
    Till the half of them were dead.
Then a stricken, weeping mother,
    Who had lost her youngest son,
Sped her to the Rabbi,† crying,
    " Save, oh, save my eldest son."
" Woman! " said the Rabbi sadly,
    " Am I God, to do this thing?

---

* F. P. Kopta: *Chronik von Böhmen,* Prague, 1852.
† The Rabbi's name was Löw.

Much as I have loved my pupil,
   Can I save him from death's sting?"
" Oh, Rabbiner," said the woman,
   " You are learned and very wise,
And Jehovah loves, your master,
   He will listen to your sighs."
" Woman! for the good of Israel
   Will you sacrifice your son?"
But the woman started backward,
   Clasping to her heart her son.
" 'Twas revealed me in a vision,"
   The learned Rabbi sadly said,
" For the crying sins of Israel,
   See our little ones are dead.
'Twas revealed me in a vision,
   All our dearest ones must die,
Till some woman gives her darling,
   Gives him up without a sigh.
To the graveyard they must lead him,
   Leave him there amidst the graves;
He will see strange sights and visions,
   Hiding where the tall grass waves;
He will see the children dancing,
   Dancing in their shrouds of lawn;
In and out amidst the stone heaps,
   They will dance their dance forlorn.
He must creep, and creep still onward,
   Till he nears the dancing band;
Then with fearless heart unshaking,
   Seize a shroud with skillful hand,
Seize a shroud and bring it to me,
   Then the pestilence will cease.
Woman, is thy heart so holy
   Thou canst give thy son in peace?"
Weeping from the Rabbi's presence,
   Went that mother stricken sore.
" Oh, Jehovah, spare my children;
   Spare the little son I bore!"
When the evening shadows lengthened,
   Lo, a girl died in her arms,
And the morrow found her weeping,
   Her dead baby's little charms.

Then the broken-hearted mother,
　Weeping, led her eldest born
To the Rabbi, saying sadly,
　" Take him—let me die forlorn!
Better he should die for Israel,
　If Jehovah will it so,
Than sink down beside the others,
　Who are lying still and low." '
" Woman!" said the Rabbi, raising
　Both his hands above her head,
" May Jehovah spare thy eldest,
　For the words that thou hast said.
Like to Abraham, who offered
　Isaac with a perfect heart,
May Jehovah spare thy darling,.
　Reunite thee ne'er to part."
When the evening shadows gathered
　In the graveyard sad and lone,
Lo, the Jewish boy was watching,
　Hid behind a mighty stone.
And at midnight all the children
　Rose as the Rabbi had said,
Dancing in their shrouds of linen
　Till the midnight hour had fled.
Then the Jewish boy soft creeping,
　Caught the shroud of one near by,
Rushed away without once turning
　At the children's bitter cry;
On he fled, fled ever onward,
　Till he reached the Rabbi's home.
At his feet he lay the garment,
　Then fell senseless as a stone.
Soon the Rabbi heard a wailing,
　And a childish voice called clear:
" Give me back my shroud of linen,
　I am naked, master, dear."
" Tell me," said the Rabbin sternly,
　" For whose sins the children die?"
Then the childish voice spake clearly,
　Telling him the reason why.
Back he gave the child his garment,
　Bid him sleep in peace for aye.
Fast and penance then he ordered,
　That the plague might pass away.

JAN AMOS KOMENSKÝ (COMENIUS).*

All hail to thee, Komenský, though thy name
   Must not be honored where thy cradle stood,
Nor happy troops of children sing thy fame,
   The little ones you loved and understood.
Yes, all the world can honor thee, but those
   For whom you strove, your brothers must be still—
Forbidden by a minister, they rose,
   To do thee honor, 'gainst a tyrant's will.

Prague like a bride arrayed herself with flags,
   And windows blazed, and music played for thee,
And e'en the beggars put away their rags,
   And students dared to dream that they were free.
All hail to thee, Komenský! though thy fate
   Was but an exile's—home you never had—
Poor and a wanderer, honor came too late
   To minister to one so old and sad.

---

* On March 28th, 1892, the Bohemians wanted to celebrate the three hundredth anniversary of the birthday of the renowned pedagogue, John Amos Komenský, like the rest of the world, by making the schoolchildren free. For no reason on earth, the Austrian government forbid this celebration. In spite of this, Prague, and every city, even the castles and villages, hung out flags and illuminated the windows. I was asked to write a poem on the subject. Komenský was also Bishop of the Moravian Brethren, and exiled by Ferdinand II. with the other Protestants. The rector of the Prague University in his own right dismissed the students, and over five hundred paraded the streets, singing national songs. No parents sent their children to school, so that the teachers had to close the schools. A deputation was sent to Naarden (Holland) with a magnificent wreath to lay on his grave, which was done in the presence of hundreds of Dutch who had gone out on purpose to honor his grave.

Thine was the Christian's faith, the dauntless heart,
  That in the darkest night still dreams of dawn;
Thine was the effort, thine the glorious part,
  To help the children in a world forlorn.
Thy voice was heard in every noble cause,
  And Europe listened to Moravia's son.
In many lands you helped to make the laws,
  For schools, and scholars, till thy days were done.

Thine was the patriot's zeal, thy native tongue
  To make more rich, by works that shall not die,
And far away in foreign lands you sung
  Your burning words, that ended with a sigh.
All hail to thee, Komenský! though thy bones
  Will never rest within thy land of birth.
In Naarden is a grave that in all zones
  Will be remembered by the learned of earth.

All hail to thee, Komenský! tyrant's might
  Can never pluck the laurels from thy brow,
Nor will thy brothers let oblivion's night
  Enshroud the grave where thou art lying now.
Thou wert an exile—but thy grave shall be
  Crowned with a laurel wreath from thy dear land,
While sympathetic nations mourn to see
  The tyranny that crushes thy loved land.

All hail to thee, Komenský! homeless here,
  Thou now hast found a home in realms more fair.
An orphan—now a Father wipes the tear
  And lays the conqueror's crown upon thy hair.
What matters if thou sleep in alien soil—
  Thy grave is honored, be it where it will.
Dishonor only rests on those who toil
  To bind their fellowmen against their will.

THE BODY AND THE SOUL.

A BOHEMIAN LEGEND.

In the churchyard, by the chapel,
    A lost soul was heard disputing
With its body lying rigid,
    In its coffin calmly sleeping.
" Oh, you body, wretched body,
    In rich silks you flaunted gayly.
Wanton were your ways and pastimes—
    Now I suffer for you sadly.

" Every thing you saw you wanted—
    Every pleasure you have tasted,
Clothed in gold and costly raiments,
    See, your life was wholly wasted.
In the dance your feet were quickest,
    Where the tambourines were playing,
And the wayward youth were singing,
    Tender words, in sooth, were saying.

" At the feast the flowing goblet,
    You have emptied without number.
Never did you think of praying,
    When you lay you down to slumber.
You have danced to sweetest music—
    I must writhe in mortal anguish.
While your body sleeps there calmly,
    I in hell am doomed to languish."

Then the body answered coldly,
    " Tell me, soul, were you not with me
When I lived in wanton splendor,
    Was there anything kept from thee?"

Then the soul said, speaking sadly,
" You say truly I was with you,
But not mistress of my actions—
   They were forced upon me by you."

" Waste no time in speaking to me,"
   Said the body, growing weary;
" Let me rest and haste thee thither,
   Where the endless years stretch dreary.'
" I will go," the soul said, calmly,
   " Leaving thee to worms and foulness,
Bearing all the pains that must be,
   Till I find God's mercy endless."

THE MASTER WORK.

Our master, Rubens, on a summer's day,
   Wandering in Spain, went in a convent church,
A poor bare church, I often heard him say,
   Belonging to an order most severe.
Idly he looked around, but soon his gaze
   Was fixed upon the picture of a monk,
A dying monk—but ne'er in all his days
   Had he beheld a work of art like this;
He called his pupils, and they also gazed,
   Admiring—wondering whose this work might be.
When Thulden turning to them half amazed,
   Said slowly, " See the name was written once,
But desecrating hands have dared efface
    The name that would have shown throughout the
      land."
" Go call the prior," Rubens said, his face
   Flushed with the wrath that shown within his eyes.
The prior came, a man of many years;
   His wan white face and sunken eyes showed plain,
That life to him had been a vale of tears.
   Silent he listened to the master's praise.
" But tell me now, oh, father, whose the hand,
   The hand that painted with a master's skill,
That dying monk, and all the heavenly band?
   I fain would see his face before I die."
" He is no longer of this world, my son,"
   The monk replied, his voice was sad and low:
" No longer of this world! His days are done!"
" And could he die, and leave his name unknown?"
" His name unknown—oh, God, it cannot be—
   The hand that painted this shall never die.
Tell me his name, oh, father, I will see
   Justice be done his shade, for I am one

Not all unknown to fame—you know my name
  Is Rubens, but I tell you all to-day;
The hand that painted this hath greater fame
  Than any I have won beneath the sun."
A flush of red o'erspread the monk's pale face,
  A blaze of light burnt in the somber eyes,
Now fixed on Rubens for a moment's space,
  Then slowly faded, as he calmly said,
" He is no longer of this world, my son."
" Tell us his name," the pupils cried; " his name
Shall be remembered—his the victory won,
  Though he lie still and silent in the grave."
" Tell us his name," our master Rubens said,
" Before whose fame perhaps my own will fade.
Let us do justice to the soul that fled,
  Unknown, unhonored to the silent land."
The monk was troubled, and his trembling hands
  He folded on his breast, to still his heart,
As though afraid it might burst its bands,
  And tell the name that quivered on his lips.
" He is no longer of this world," he said,
" A convent door has closed upon his life;
He has renounced this world—see he is dead!
  Leave him in peace, my son, he is a monk."
" A monk! " said Rubens, " Oh, my father, say,
  What convent hides the man that painted this?
A genius has no right to turn away,
  And scorn the fame that would attend his steps;
I shall go to him, whisper in his ear,
  ' Fame beckons to thee, friend, come leave thy cell.'
And should he tremble, and draw back in fear,
  I will assure him of the pope's good will.
The pope he loves me, father, he will hear,
  He will absolve him from his convent vow,
And he will live among us ever near,
  Honored and loved, and reverenced by us all."
" I will not tell you what his name may be,
  Nor where he lives," the monk replied in haste.
" Leave him in peace, my son, this may not be—
  He has renounced the world and all its fame."
Then Rubens said in wrath: " The pope shall know
  What treasure you have hid in convent cell."

Believe me, father, he will quickly send
  A messenger to bring him from his cell."
" Listen to me, my son," the monk replied,
" Before this weary soul at length found cheer,
Think you he had no struggle with himself—
  Ere he renounced the world, and then came here?
Think you he left the world, its wealth, its joy,
  Before a bitter struggle had been fought.
Before he knew how idle friendships claim,
  How vain the glory that the many sought.
Striking his breast, he said, " Listen, my son,
  Leave him in peace, where peace he sought and found,
E'en earthly fame is but an idle dream,
  One sleeps as well 'neath monument or mound,
And if you saw him, mark me, he would say,
  And here he crossed himself, that God alone
Had called him to this cloister cell unknown,
  Where he in peace could for his sins atone.
And He who called him, see, my son, can give
  Strength to renounce this prospect seeming fair,
That you thrust on him, oh, I know him well,
  He would not yield but lo, he might despair."
" Yes, but my fathe   'tis an endless fame,
  That he renounces for this convent cell."
" My son, what is an endless fame on earth,
  To the eternities where God doth dwell?"
Rubens was silent, and his scholars all,
  With saddened faces, left the cloister gate.
The prior went back, and by his narrow bed
  Fell on his knees and thanked God for his fate.
Then he arose, and gathered up his paints,
  Brushes, and palette, with sad, pale face,
And threw them in the river flowing near;
  Of all his many works he left no trace.
Sadly he watched them floating far away,
  While thoughts unutterable before him swept,
And then he turned him to his crucifix,
  To seek the aid of Him "who also wept."